Also By R.W. Wallace

Short Story Collections

Mystery
Deep Dark Secrets
A Thief in the Night
Unfinished Business

Young Adult
Tales From the Trenches

Ghost Detective Series
Beyond the Grave
Unveiling the Past
Beneath the Surface
Piercing the Veil

Author of the Ghost Detective Series

R.W. WALLACE

HEARTWARMING HOLIDAY TALES

A HOLIDAY SHORT STORY
COLLECTION

Heartwarming Holiday Tales
by R.W. Wallace

"The Magic of Sharing" Copyright © 2020 by R.W. Wallace
First published in WMG's 2020 Holiday Spectacular
"Down the Memory Aisle" Copyright © 2021 by R.W. Wallace
"Morbier Impossible" Copyright © 2020 by R.W. Wallace
"A Second Chance" Copyright © 2020 by R.W. Wallace
"Severed Ties" Copyright © 2021 by R.W. Wallace
First published in Pulphouse Fiction Magazine Issue #15

Cover by R.W. Wallace
Cover Illustration 58200883 © rakchai | Depositphotos

All characters and events in this book, other than those clearly in the public domain, are fictitious and any resemblance to real persons, living or dead, is purely coincidental.

All rights reserved. No part of this publication may be reproduced, distributed, or transmitted in any form or by any means, including photocopying, recording, or other electronic or mechanical methods, without the prior written permission of the publisher, except in the case of brief quotations embodied in critical reviews and certain other noncommercial uses permitted by copyright law.

www.rwwallace.com

ISBN paperback: [978-2-493670-11-3]
ISBN ebook: [978-2-493670-12-0]

First Edition

TABLE OF CONTENTS

Introduction	1
The Magic of Sharing	3
Down the Memory Aisle	19
Morbier Impossible	37
A Second Chance	55
Severed Ties	73
Author's Note	102
About the Author	103
Also by R.W. Wallace	104

Introduction

My first holiday-themed book! If you'd told me a few years ago that I'd be putting one of these out, I wouldn't have believed you. While I enjoy reading holiday stories, I'd have sworn I didn't have it in me to write one.

Of course, I also swore I'd never write a short story, so I've basically stopped making firm statements like that. Clearly, I know nothing.

In 2020 (less than a month before the world shut down and my last social interaction in way too long), I participated in my first WMG Anthology Workshop and found myself faced with the challenge of writing three holiday stories in quick succession.

Well, I had to turn in *something*, didn't I?

I discovered I *did* have some holiday stories in me — and that I enjoyed writing them. I just needed to remember what I loved about that time of the year.

At first, my brain clearly associated holidays with Norway — where I grew up and celebrated many, many happy holidays

— but since, I've figured out how to set some of them in France, too. In fact, in this volume, I believe three are set in France, and only two in Norway! You'll note the really cute ones are in the snow in Norway, though.

While all the stories in this volume tend toward the heartwarming variety, they are in no way similar. It goes from Scandinavian nisse dreaming of porridge, to a sweet romance, to mice with parachutes on a mission, and Christmas trees with stories to tell. And a Ghost Detective story, of course. Robert and Clothilde can figure out how to fit in anywhere.

I hope you'll find something to your tastes!

Enjoy!

R.W. Wallace
www.rwwallace.com

THE MAGIC OF SHARING

In the freezing Norwegian countryside, a family of nisse watches the humans celebrate Christmas on their farm, with delicious dishes and shiny presents — as human tradition dictates.

The nisse long to join in the festivities, watching quietly from outside as the farm's occupants celebrate. Without real hope, they wonder if the humans will remember the nisse tradition.

The nisse don't need food to survive or presents to be happy. They need someone to believe in them.

The Magic of Sharing is a tale of hope and sharing — porridge and sleds included!

The Magic of Sharing

Three cold noses pressed up against the windowpane, we watch as the family finishes off their Christmas dinner. There's nothing but bones left of the smoked and salted lamb—the *pinnekjøtt*—someone left half a potato in the dish and both the father and mother have been eying it but seem to decide they really are too full, and the three-year-old seems to think Christmas has come an hour early because he's allowed to finish off the dish of mashed rutabaga with his fingers.

The parents have finished two bottles of Christmas beer each—the kind with *nisser* on them, making the fact that we're out here starving just a little bit worse—while the kids are drinking *julebrus*, the red soda that's only available this time of year.

Toward the back of the room, the fireplace is quietly crackling in one corner and the Christmas tree calmly waiting its turn in the other.

They went all out with the tree this year. They always pick one out from their own forest, but since the ultimate goal of that forest is for the trees to grow tall and straight to be cut down and sold, they usually take one of the feeble ones, one that won't bring in a profit later. This usually means that their Christmas tree is halfway dead, twisted, or maimed in some way.

The tree currently in the corner almost reaches the ceiling, is straight as an arrow, and has branches on all sides. The look the mother gave the father when he brought it in made me think this was his early present for his wife—their tree was going to be a beauty this year.

The entire family spent yesterday morning decorating it. The father put in the lights and the star on the top. The mother did the Norwegian flags, the tinsel, and the breakable decorations.

The three kids did all the rest: woven baskets, angels, nisser, baubles, and some unidentifiable ones that they'd made themselves.

All the while, we were standing out here in the cold, looking in.

Nissemor, my wife, can't seem to stop staring at the tree. She's always had a weak spot for the lights, loving how they give the entire room a soft glow at night when everyone has gone to bed. They remind her of the open starry sky, which she can spend hours gazing at when the weather allows. Here, they're in a setting that screams of the love this family has for each other and the holiday. Anything representing love has Nissemor's heart.

Tulla, my daughter, has her eyes on the presents. Not because she wants to open them—we nisser have never had any use for the toys, clothes, or books inside those packets—but because she's anticipating the moment the children will open them. Tulla loves playing, loves a good prank, loves anything that will make a child scream in joy. And those colorfully packaged gifts always deliver.

"Is it time for the presents now, Dad?" Her face is squished into the window to the point where her nose is completely flat and even her lips and forehead are pressed to the glass.

"They've finished eating, so it's time for the presents, right?" She places her palms on the glass and closes her eyes. "Please, please, please," she whispers fervently. I put a hand on her shoulder, giving it a little squeeze. "They'll get to the presents, Tulla." I swallow a gulp. "They haven't had dessert yet."

Her knitted red hat and matching sweater are covered in snow from when she made a snow angel on the roof earlier. Her gray felt pants are probably wet but so long as she doesn't complain, I won't say a thing.

Nissemor tears her gaze away from the tree and we share a look. This is always the most painful part of the night for us.

This used to be *our* moment.

We nisser don't really need human food to sustain ourselves. Well, no, we do. But we don't need the humans to *give* it to us, we just help ourselves. We're no bigger than your regular house cat and don't need much to get by, so the humans never notice if one potato goes missing here and one piece of cheese is suddenly a little smaller there.

What we do need is their belief in us.

And that has been waning dangerously over the last few years.

On the farm next door, the Jensen family, there used to be a nisse family much like ours. They lived in the hayloft and helped out mostly with the cattle. Their young son, especially, had a way with the calves that had saved more than one life. Then, five years ago, the humans had their own son, a squealing and loud thing they named Ole.

The year Ole turned two, they decorated the entire barn with Christmas lights, adding more as they saw how much the little boy loved them. When he turned three, they added a Santa Claus with a sleigh. The kid *adored* the reindeer.

Last year, they got a neighbor to dress up as Santa and bring gifts.

We haven't seen the nisse family since.

We don't need much but we need their belief. And the ultimate show of faith comes on Christmas Eve.

In the good old days, everybody knew the drill. Be nice to the nisse on Christmas Eve and give him his porridge, and he'll help you out around the farm the entire year. Don't give him his food, and he'll do the opposite. He'll mess with the animals, move your hay over to your neighbor's barn, make sure the crops don't grow.

I haven't pulled any mean tricks like that since I was a kid. Haven't dared to.

Despite not having had porridge in over twenty years.

But they still remember us. They at least *sort of* believe. Which is why we're still here.

Inside the house, the mother is preparing the dessert in the kitchen while the father takes a seat on the couch, the children settling in around him.

"Oh, they're going to read the story!" Tulla does a quick pirouette before squeezing her nose back to the window.

Indeed, they're reading the story. The one about the nisse and the fox, where the nisse convinces the fox not to steal any of the humans' chickens on Christmas Eve. Where he shares his porridge with the animal instead.

It's a sweet story—and probably why we're still here. The question is how long it'll last.

I put my arms around Nissemor as we watch the father turn the pages and the children's reactions. The six-year-old daughter, especially, seems completely caught up in the story and frequently stops her father to ask questions.

When the story is done, the dessert is on the table. Like every year, it's rice pudding, made from porridge and whipped cream.

The father gives the mother a kiss before sitting down. The oldest starts sprinkling his dessert with sugar. The youngest puts his hand directly into his plate, earning him a half-hearted rebuke from both parents.

The six-year-old doesn't take her seat. She stands next to her chair, staring at the plate.

"Why aren't they eating?" Tulla whispers. "They have to eat, so they can finish eating, so they can get to the presents. That big one in the back is a sled, I'm sure of it!"

The girl doesn't move, even when her mother clearly tells her to take her seat so they can all have their dessert.

A discussion ensues, apparently having something to do with the rice pudding. I wish I could hear what they're saying, but the only way to hear them is by going through the attic, and that would mean missing out on too much.

The mother's frustration seems to grow as the daughter

refuses to comply, but I notice the father's features softening. When his wife is clearly about to lose her temper, he shoots one quick glance at the couch—where the storybook was discarded—and gets up from his seat.

He takes his daughter into the kitchen. They get a plate. Fill it with porridge. They heat it in the microwave. Sprinkle with sugar and cinnamon. And the daughter puts the biggest dollop of butter I have ever seen in the very center.

"Is that...?" Nissemor has a hand over her mouth and her breath hitches.

I'm afraid to get my hopes up.

"What are they *doing*?" Tulla says. "Why do they need porridge on top of the rice pudding? Can't they just eat? Get to the gifts already?"

Tulla was born the year of our last portion of porridge. She has never tasted it, not the real thing, the one given to us by humans. She doesn't understand the significance, as she's never felt the magic of real belief. She has spent her entire life in this half-life existence we've had for the last twenty years.

Could it really be...?

Nissemor and I both hold our breaths as the father tells his daughter to put on her winter jacket and snowshoes, then gently places the bowl of porridge in her hands before opening the front door for her.

"She's going to do it," Nissemor whispers in awe.

The father closes the door behind his daughter and walks over to our window to keep an eye on her. We jump down from our spot to hide next to a pile of firewood. The humans usually can't see us anyway but it's best to always play it safe.

"What's going on?" Tulla whispers.

"You'll see," I tell her. "Just keep quiet, darling, and you'll see."

The girl very carefully walks to the barn, the porridge steaming in her hands and her lips set in a thin line as she focuses on not spilling any. Her breath comes out in short puffs of steam.

She places the plate by the barn door. From her pocket, she pulls out a wooden spoon and puts it in the plate. "There," she says. "Now you won't be hungry. Merry Christmas, nisser." And she runs back to the house.

In the window, the father follows his daughter with his eyes, a fond smile on his lips.

"She gave us porridge," Nissemor says, her voice shaking with emotion. "Porridge!"

Tulla's gaze goes from me to her mother, clearly confused but also understanding that she's missing something significant.

I take both their hands and pull them over to the steaming plate. "Come," I tell them. "Let's eat while it's still warm. Oh, look at that butter. I don't think I've ever had that much of it before, even in my youth. Would you like to taste it, Tulla?"

For the first time in twenty years, we have our Christmas feast. Our bellies are full of porridge, sugar, and butter, and our hearts full of love and belief.

We're so engrossed in our meal, we miss most of the unpacking of the gifts. When Tulla remembers it, she lurches toward the window, high on butter. She makes a tiny greasy handprint on the glass as she squints toward the Christmas tree.

"It's a sled! I knew it! She's going to have so much fun with that." She burps and seems on the point of falling asleep on her feet.

Nissemor walks up to her. "Maybe it's time for you to go to—"

"She's coming out to test it! She's going to ride the sled straight away! Yesss!"

Tulla takes off toward the front door, sleepiness long forgotten.

"What if one of them sees her?" Nissemor frowns in worry.

"They won't," I tell her. "And if they do, the parents will blame the alcohol and the kids won't really know it's not normal." In any case, they can only see us if they believe in us, so I've been walking around in broad daylight for years. Not that I've ever told Nissemor about it. No need to cause her unnecessary worry.

Two minutes later, the girl comes out the front door, wrapped up in thick winter coveralls, a red bonnet, a blue scarf, and red mittens. She's pulling the brand new red plastic sled behind her and beelines directly for the road. The farm is at the end of the road so there's no risk of any cars coming and the first fifty meters or so are downhill with the perfect incline for a six-year-old to ride her sled.

Tulla runs after her, not wanting to miss a single moment of the fun.

Inside the barn, I hear one of the cows low, in a tone I don't like very much.

"Why don't you go keep an eye on Tulla," I tell Nissemor. "I'm going to check on the
cows."

It's Dagros, one of the oldest cows in the barn. She's expecting and the calf is due any day now. In fact, I'm tempted to say it's already on its way.

But something's wrong. The cows, and especially one as experienced as Dagros, know how to give birth on their own. The sounds she's making right now make me think she *doesn't* know what's going on—and that's a bad sign.

I try to help her as well as I can and do my best to calm her but her complaining only gets louder.

I need to get help. I give Dagros a last reassurance before going to the barn door. The thing is very big and heavy for a small nisse like myself but with some effort, I do manage to get it open.

I don't need it open for *me*, of course. I have my secret passages all over the farm. But I know what the humans consider worrisome and worthy of investigation. The barn door standing wide open on a winter night definitely qualifies.

Next, I open the front door. I jump up to grab and lower the handle, then give the door a big push so it slams open.

Then I run and hide in the bushes.

It doesn't take the father more than ten seconds to come to the door. He pokes his head out and yells, "Marie, you know you have to take care with the door…" When his daughter is nowhere in sight and he hears her joyful screams from down the road, he frowns and pokes his head farther outside to try to figure out what caused his door to bang open.

He sees the open barn door. Swears. Closes the door, but comes back out less than a minute later, with a coat and boots on.

I run ahead of him inside the barn and into Dagros's stall.

"Come now, Dagros. Moo loudly for the human, will you? He'll be able to help you."

It works. Dagros is louder than ever, and the human comes to check on her instead of just shutting the barn door.

I make a very quick appearance, just to check my theory. There's no reaction from the man, even though I was in his line of sight, so he really can't see me. For this situation, that's a good thing. It means I don't have to keep out of sight.

While the man first goes inside to change, then comes back out and helps the calf get into the right position, I work on calming the cow. She's stressed out about the birth not going like the previous ones, worried about her unborn calf, and in a lot of pain.

Contrary to the people, she *can* see me, and my presence helps. She doesn't kick out at the man who's helping her or step on his feet, which I consider a success.

At one point, I see Nissemor in the barn door, looking rather distressed, but when she sees how busy I am, she turns around and doesn't interrupt us.

An hour later, a beautiful female calf is born. The calf is exhausted, Dagros is exhausted, the man is barely able to stand on his own. But everyone is alive and healthy.

"You go on back to your family," I say softly. "Dagros and I can take it from here."

The man doesn't hear me, not exactly, but he listens anyway. Five minutes later, he's back inside the house, probably getting a shower, while I help Dagros take care of her newborn.

Nissemor comes back to the barn. There's a sheen of sweat on her face and her voice is shaking. "Nissefar," she says. "Please come."

The Magic of Sharing

I can't remember if I've ever heard her so afraid before. "What's wrong?" I run out of Dagros's stall and take her in my arms. "Is Tulla okay?"

She shakes her head and breaks out of my embrace, pulls me after her by my hand. "Come see."

As we reach the road, I catch sight of the girl driving down the slope on her sled. She lets out a whoop of joy that must be heard all the way down in the village. I look around, searching for Tulla, who logically shouldn't be very far when one of the kids is having this much fun.

"Where is she?" I ask. "Did something happen to her?" Helping Dagros was important but if Tulla was in danger, getting her out of trouble was *more* important.

Nissemor points down the road, at the sled that has just come to a stop.

The girl gets out of the sled. Holds out a hand—to help Tulla get out.

"She can see her?"

"She not only sees her," Nissemor cries. "She talks to her, touches her, *plays* with her! What are we going to do?"

I'm speechless. I just stand there, watching, as the two children make their way up the hill, the sled trailing behind them. They're *chatting*, the girl gesticulating and Tulla skipping along as if having the time of her life.

"Humans aren't allowed to see nisser," Nissemor says. "What do we do?"

I have no idea.

Then again, who's going to come punish us because a human

has seen a nisse? It's not like there's a police for it.

The two girls approach and I step into the shadows of a nearby tree. Nissemor doesn't move.

"She can only see Tulla," Nissemor says.

"Oh." I ease back to stand next to my wife.

The girls get back on the sled, the human girl sheltering our Tulla between her legs, and back down the slope they go, whooping all the way.

"What are they talking about?" I ask.

"They spent about half an hour on the porridge," Nissemor says. "Then another half hour on the other gifts the girl got, with Tulla making suggestions for their use that the parents are *not* going to like. And now they're trying to always drive down the same tracks, to make them as icy as possible, in order to increase their speed."

"Okay." I don't know what else to say.

౷

SOME TIME LATER, as Orion sits just above the barn and the white owl from down the valley has flown past with two different mice in its beak, the front door opens and the mother comes out to get her daughter back inside.

"But I don't want to, Mamma! I'm having too much fun with the nisse."

The mother chuckles as she stands at the top of the slope, her arms around herself, hands in her armpits, trying to stay warm. "That's great, darling, but it's getting really late and it's time to go to bed. Pappa is already asleep. Did you know Dagros had her calf?"

"She did?" This makes the girl pause. She looks to Tulla. "Did you know about this?"

Tulla shakes her head. "I was here with you, remember?"

"Who are you talking to?" the mother asks.

"The nisse, of course! Told you I was playing with her."

"Okay." With a fond smile, the mother takes the sled and pulls it up to the house. The daughter follows.

"Tulla," I call to my daughter. "You can't risk being seen by anyone else, darling. The game must end here."

She isn't happy about it but she understands. She must know that what happened here tonight was exceptional.

Tulla pulls on the human girl's leg to get her to stop. The girl bends down and the two have a short discussion. The girl looks our way several times, likely because Tulla says we're here, but she can't actually see us. Finally, she nods in acceptance and bends down to give my daughter a hug.

Then she follows her mother inside.

It's just us three nisser, out in the cold winter night, with a sky full of stars and the moon reflecting in the snow, and the weak lowing of the new calf in the barn. We're pretty much in the same situation as we were earlier, staring longingly in at the humans and their holiday feast.

Except we've also had ours. We've eaten enough porridge and butter to last us till next Christmas. We'll keep helping with the animals, getting rid of the rodents. Do our parts around the farm.

And in return, we'll hope that next Christmas, we'll once again get that little taste of magic.

DOWN THE MEMORY AISLE

*Like a house full of filing cabinets, our minds offer
easy access to certain memories — your best friend's
smile, the name of your favorite chocolate cake...*

*Other memories prove more elusive, perhaps
stored in a cellar or forgotten corridor.*

But they're all there. Nothing is forgotten.

*The simple nudge of a frosty day and a familiar stroll may
be all we need to bring lovely recollections from the deepest files
and create space where fresh moments will be forever saved.*

Down the Memory Aisle

Memory's an odd thing. It's like your mind is made up of endless walls of filing cabinets, every file a separate memory. Some are easily accessible, in the main aisles where you walk down every day, the cabinet drawers sliding open easily on well-greased rails, and the sheets filed into sections that you know by heart so you don't even need to look to pull out the right one.

The names of your best friends, right there on the left. The color of your childhood bedroom, up there in the right hand corner. The name of your favorite chocolate cake from the bakery downstairs, down here, close to the floor, filed next to the price of pasta and a romantic date from last year. Don't bother trying to understand. It makes sense to me, that's all that matters.

Some files are always here, on the main aisle, but can't quite decide where their place is. Like the car keys. On the table by the door? In the ignition? In the pants I just threw in the wash? It's one of the three. If I can't remember which one, I'll just open all three cabinets.

It's very rare for a file to completely disappear. If I heard something, said something, lived something, I *will* remember it if someone nudges me in the right direction. *You know, we were in that seafood restaurant in Bergen and it was absolutely pouring outside. A foreigner tried to use an umbrella and it was thrown into the fjord. Remember that dress you were wearing? It was fabulous.* Oh, right. Down the third corridor on the right, I think, then down a flight of stairs and…there! I have to put all my weight into pulling the drawer open, squeaking all the way. But there, in the next-to-last folder, is the fabulous blue dress I wore that night. I spilled red wine down the front just before leaving and could never get it clean. If I had to, I could probably find the file on what I did with the dress, but that's not the point here.

The point is, the mind is vast. And some hallways—hell, entire floors—we don't walk down for years. We know it's there, and it's not a scary place or anything, we just haven't had an excuse to visit. Nobody switched on a light, reminding us of the elevator. Nobody offered to play hide-and-seek in the stacks.

So when you do remember all those memories you stored away, it can be a bit of a shock. Switch on the light and realize it's not just a light bulb dangling from the ceiling, but a sparkling chandelier. The filing cabinets aren't straight rows of boring black like on the main aisle, but a jumble of blue and red and orange, not a one the same size or design as its neighbor, files poking out of hastily closed drawers or lying discarded on the psychedelically carpeted floor.

If you'd thought about it, you'd have known there were several rooms, but you always only glanced at the closest two in passing. The dozens and dozens of rooms farther back never even showed up on your GPS in the past decade.

And now, because of one missed bus, I'm back on that crazy teen-aged carpet. All the lights are on, I remember the alleys in the back and the cozy loveseat around the corner. Or maybe I should say freezing park bench…

I don't come back to Trondheim very often. I grew up here and spent my first eighteen years trudging up and down the hills surrounding the city center. School, soccer, handball, choir, cross country skiing, hanging out with friends. All the usual stuff. I wasn't one of the cool kids, but neither was I one of the uncool ones. More the average girl that nobody really noticed.

Except the one guy who did.

See, that's the revelation that has me literally freezing my ass off on a park bench in the middle of the night two days after Christmas.

I'd forgotten about Magnus. Somehow. When I tell someone about my formative years in Trondheim, he never even comes to mind. I'll talk about my choice of high school and my grades, my naive hopes for the future. I'll mention my group of friends, which has somehow managed to keep in touch for over a decade, despite two of us having moved to a different part of the country. I'll even recount the memorable soccer match where we lost 17-0, the day I admitted to myself I'd never be a great player and should perhaps try out some other sports. Something with less running after a ball.

But I never mention, because I never think of, the boy who made me feel special one night in December my senior year in high school.

We were sitting right here, on this bench, both of us shaking from equal parts laughter and cold, when he kissed me. Said he'd been watching me, that he liked me.

I still have trouble believing it.

I had negotiated for hours with my parents to be allowed to go to the party at my friend Kathrine's place on December 26th. Traditionally, Christmas Eve is celebrated with family. Christmas Mass, Christmas dinner, Christmas gifts, Christmas beer… The salmon is for Christmas Day, and it's still a family affair. Then, after two whole days of family, there's a need for some time off, so on the 26th, it's time to party—with friends.

But alcohol is usually abundant at these parties, even the ones with participants under the legal age of eighteen, and my parents weren't very keen on letting me go. I think the only reason they let me was that I could legally drink, so their arguments were moot. I'd been eighteen for two whole months, and had yet to come home drunk. At some point, they'd have to start trusting me.

They did blindside me a little, though. At the time, I was furious, but as the events of the evening unfolded, they were easily forgiven. Since the party was several kilometers from our house, they didn't want me to be walking around alone at night. So they arranged for a boy who was going to the same party, and just happened to be the son of one of my dad's colleagues, to accompany me.

They got me a babysitter.

I was still screaming my head off at my mother when he knocked on our door. Feeling more attached to my reputation (or lack thereof) than to putting my mother in her place, I stopped complaining and promised my parents there would be *words* the next day. Took some pleasure in using that expression on them. I opened the front door and found myself face-to-face with an uncertain smile and gentle green eyes.

"You're Emma?" Magnus said. Although he was clearly nervous, there was a self-assurance about him that I liked. Not arrogance, far from it, but he wasn't the type who would fold immediately if he met resistance.

I recognized him. He'd been a year ahead of me, so was probably off studying something or other now. Didn't know much more, though.

A glance at my mother showed she was way too interested for comfort. No way was I giving her anything after the surprise she'd just sprung on me. "Yep, that's me," I said. "Let's go." I grabbed my coat, jumped into my boots, and off we went.

Trondheim center is at sea level, with the fjord on one side and the Nidelva river slinging around to cover the rest. Bakklandet, where our party was held, is a small neighborhood made up of cutesy, colorful, and ancient wooden houses on the north side of the river, squeezed in between the cold river and the hills rising toward where I lived. The slope is quite steep and the bike elevator has been the source of many articles and travel blogs.

That's not the steepest climb, though. That comes at the very top, just before reaching the spot housing the local radio tower on Tyholt.

In excellent Norwegian style, someone figured the fastest route from A to B was a straight line, so they made a road go right down from top to bottom. Then they also made a zig-zagging grid of normally sloped roads throughout the hillside, allowing the inhabitants to get in and out without risking life and limbs every time.

I'm sure it won't surprise anybody to learn that nobody below the age of twenty would ever consider choosing the zig-zags over the straight line, be it to go up or down, in summer or winter, on foot or by bike. We all have winter tires, after all.

Tonight I'm going up the infamous climb, away from the city center. But back then, on that magical night, we had to go *down* the steep descent. And it was covered in ice. We'd been lucky enough to have a white Christmas on the 24th, then on the 25th, everything started to melt. Only to freeze again on the 26th. So the roads that hadn't been a first priority for the snow plows were covered in a ten centimeter thick layer of iced slush.

We'd stopped at the top to consider our options. At this point, we'd been walking and talking for twenty minutes and were becoming comfortable with each other. Magnus had told me about his first year studying Physics at the university in Oslo and I'd recounted all the ridiculous drama surrounding my friends in school. I was comfortable talking to him and was already looking forward to walking back home with him after the party.

"There's no way we're making it down the slope without falling on our asses at least five times," Magnus said. The ice was so smooth, the moonlight reflected a perfect image up at us.

Laid out below us, Trondheim by night. The cathedral towered over everything else with its stone facade and tall green spire. The old white fort built to defend against attackers coming in the fjord was beautifully lit up at the bottom of the steep incline, halfway down the hill. And the dark expanse of the fjord on the right. Breathing in the crisp December air, I reveled in the magic of it all.

Taking the sensible route down didn't sound very magical. Or fun. It *would* buy me more time alone with Magnus, but I'd need more to step down from the challenge he'd issued.

"Five times?" I scoffed. "How old and scared are you? It's all about confidence. You accept the fact you'll slip and go with it. I say two falls, max, when we slide off the road, and, you know, possibly when we need to slow down." We'd cross the zig-zagging roads several times but the chances of meeting cars were slim to none. On the large road at the bottom, though…

"You're proposing we slide down in one go?" Magnus's smile said he was game, but his tone gave away his apprehension.

I couldn't stop grinning. Couldn't remember the last time I'd had so much fun. "There's two of us. If we hold onto each other, we'll have four feet. Should be pretty stable."

"As a student in Physics, I'd like to point out that your logic most likely won't hold up against reality." But he was scoping out the slope below us, picking out the dangerous spots, the greatest challenges.

"Ah!" I held up a gloved finger. "Most likely. Where there's uncertainty, there's hope."

"That's not how the saying goes."

Shrugging, I checked my coat was securely closed, that all my pockets were sealed, that my phone was safely tucked away against my breast. I flashed my best smile and looked straight into his beautiful green eyes. "You scared?"

He couldn't back down now.

Standing at the very edge of the downward slope, we took up wide stances and grabbed each other's elbows. It felt pretty stable.

Until we gave a push and set off down the slope. That ice was *smooth*. We gained speed even faster than when rolling down here on a bike in summer without using the brakes. Which is to mean, *fast*.

We were lucky our aim wasn't better. If we'd managed to stay in the middle of the road, we'd have ended up going fast enough to break something when we inevitably fell. As it were, we only made it to the first zig-zag. By then, we'd gotten turned around at least a dozen times already and my head was spinning. All my energy and focus went into staying on my feet and holding onto Magnus for dear life. When we hit that other road, the gravel we hadn't incorporated into our calculations tripped us up.

I lost my footing but kept hold of Magnus. He emitted a loud *oof* when I landed on his chest and then a grunt when we slid into the ditch.

"Ouch," he groaned. "Told you we wouldn't make it." He chuckled.

I couldn't believe I'd done something so crazy. It was totally unlike me. But it was so much *fun*! I started giggling uncontrollably, which didn't help in the least with catching my breath.

"Can I assume you're not hurt?" Magnus asked. He was lying flat in the ditch, making for a comfortable mattress for me. His back must have been freezing, though.

"I'm fine," I managed. "You didn't break anything? I wonder what my parents would say if I broke the babysitter?"

"As long as I don't get blamed for breaking the baby, everything's fine." He anticipated my slug and held up his arms to protect his face. His whole body vibrated as he laughed.

With a lot of slipping, a couple of accidental knees to Magnus's midsection, and a fair amount of swearing, we made it out of the ditch and onto the grassy patch on the side of the road. Right next to the park bench.

"I need a break," Magnus said between pants. He was bent in half, his gloved hands on his knees and his back and thighs covered in snow and dirt. His hair was flattened to the back of his head and his cheeks rosy red from cold and exertion.

I couldn't take my eyes off him.

"There's a bench right here, old man," I teased him. "I'll wait while you catch your breath." I sat down on the freezing bench and patted the seat next to me.

We stayed long after he'd caught his breath. The seat was so cold, I soon couldn't feel my ass anymore, and I couldn't care less. My entire focus was on the boy next to me, on his stories, his smile. I wanted to stay there all night.

At one point, a guy in his thirties passed us slowly on his bike. Even on the zig-zags, only the most sporty ones manage the entire climb without stepping off the bike. We sat and watched him in silence until he disappeared over the hill.

I turned back to Magnus, expecting him to say we should get going to the party. Instead, he was much closer than before, his green eyes intense. "I really like you," he said. "Always thought you looked like a great girl and I'm happy to discover I was right."

I had no comeback. I stared wide-eyed at the sincerity of his expression, not quite able to comprehend he was saying this so seriously. My gaze dropped to his lips, which might be what got him moving.

Suddenly, his lips were on mine, one of his hands grabbing mine in my lap. We were both frozen but his breath was warm.

How could I have forgotten the memory of my sweetest kiss ever?

Well, not forgotten exactly. Hidden away in a colorful filing cabinet on a side aisle.

We never made it to the party. By the time we were too cold to stay there and keep kissing, it was almost two in the morning and we decided to turn our noses homeward instead. We walked slowly, holding hands, stopping frequently to kiss some more.

Maybe the fact it was a one-night thing is why I haven't thought back on it much. We didn't make any plans to meet up after we made it home. I guess it would have broken the magic of the moment. A couple of days later, Magnus went back to Oslo to study, and I continued being the girl nobody noticed.

And here I am again. A party on December 26th, slippery white roads, a slope to conquer. Except this time I'm alone and I'm going up instead of down. I've done at least eighty percent of the work already and I don't really need a break.

But it's the same bench.

My ass is frozen through. Trondheim by night is blinking up at me and a large catamaran is speeding away from the docks toward the mouth of the fjord. The faint sound of cars rises from the road down by the fort, but this area is empty and quiet. I'm supposed to be meeting my friends from high school and pretend we're eighteen again while drinking grownup drinks but I'd rather sit here and remember the boy who'd noticed me. Who thought I was special.

I keep saying I don't have many happy memories from high school. No miserable ones either, but I generally feel like I missed out on something intangible. Except maybe I didn't. I've just chosen not to think about any of it in years, good or bad.

I think I'll sit here and think about it now. A trip down the colorfully carpeted memory aisle. Enjoy the sparkling chandelier.

The squeaky crunch of someone walking on the frozen snow on the sidewalk breaks into my thoughts. Another lonely party-goer?

A lanky man with a beanie pulled down over his ears is trudging up the steep incline I climbed earlier. No zig-zags for this guy. He sees me sitting here and there's a hitch in his step.

He stops when he's on a level with my bench. Should I worry about being out here all alone in the middle of the night?

"I wondered if you might be invited to the same party. Home for the holidays, Emma?"

My jaw drops. I scramble to lean forward to get a better look at his face. "Magnus?"

Even surrounded by a trimmed blond beard and with the youthful roundness of his cheeks long gone, there's no mistaking the smile. It's too dark for me to make out the color of his eyes but I realize I don't need to—my memory remembers them perfectly.

"Was the climb too long for you? Getting lazy in your old age?"

I'm grinning from ear to ear. It's like my walk down memory lane took me back in time. Same place, same date, same weather, same guy. And yet it's different. I'm not the uncertain girl I was at eighteen. I've gained experience, lost innocence, learned about life.

And even through my adult lens, Magnus looks great. The boy he was back then, and the man he is now.

I plan to make a witty retort, show him I haven't lost my touch. Instead, I blurt out the truth. "I remembered our night here and stopped for a moment of nostalgia."

His smile softens. "Nostalgia is positive, right? So that's a good sign?" I scoot over on the bench and Magnus sits down, one elbow on the backrest as he faces me.

It never even occurs to me to hold back. We only knew each other for a night but it was enough for me to trust him not to hurt me if I'm honest. "That night was magical and holds nothing but positive memories for me."

"Oh, good. I was worried you might be mad I didn't try to keep in touch or anything."

I sit on my hands to keep from reaching out to touch him. Just because I've been reliving the memory of fifteen years ago doesn't mean he's in the same state of mind. "I could have reached out too. Maybe the memory was too perfect for a follow-up."

Magnus hums but I'm not sure it's in agreement. "I thought about reaching out. No, really! But I was in Oslo, you were here. We were just kids." He chuckles. "And you're probably right about not wanting to ruin a perfect memory."

"I'll have you know I'm always right." I lift my nose in the air.

"Sure you are. You were certainly right about us being able to slide down the hill without hiccups."

We burst out laughing.

As a comfortable silence settles, I sneak a glance at Magnus out of the corner of my eye. And am promptly busted because Magnus isn't pretending not to stare.

"What?" I say, my voice a little shaky. "Do I have something on my face?"

I can see the cheeky retorts lining up in his eyes. But he voices none of them. Just smiles at me.

"I found you on Facebook," he says. "Yeah, yeah, I know, very stalkerish. But from time to time something makes me think of Trondheim and I invariably end up thinking about you."

Wow, thinking about the city makes him go straight to me? I'm not sure if I should be worried or flattered. Maybe a little of both.

"So I looked you up. Saw you also live in Bergen and was *so* close to clicking that friend button."

My head whips around. "*Also?*"

His smile has a hint of uncertainty now. "I've been living in Bergen for five years. I work at the university."

I just sit there gaping. We've been living in the same city for five years? Somehow, even though I never thought about him, it feels like we missed out. We could have had so much fun.

Magnus clears his throat. "I think it's about time for me to point out I'm not here tonight because I'm stalking you. I'm honest to god invited to the same party. But I knew the friend who invited me is a friend of your friend, so…" His wince is kind of cute.

It's time I save him from the awkwardness. "I'm sorry I didn't stalk you back," I say with a smile. "I'm thinking maybe I should have."

I think about my friends. They're probably already drunkenly looking at pictures from our glory days and promising they'll meet up more often than once a year from now on. I'm sure it's loads of fun and I *do* want to meet my friends again. But I want to stay here even more, frozen ass and all.

"Will anyone miss you if you don't show up at that party tonight?" I ask.

Magnus cocks an eyebrow. "Are you asking me if my friends maybe won't notice if I'm not there? I am *not* invisible."

I take it as an invitation to give him a once-over. I take my time about it, too. "I know you're not." I nod toward the steep climb behind him. "But we never finished our descent. You up for a challenge? Or have you gotten scared in your old age?"

His smile lights up the cold winter night and his eyes sparkle like emeralds. "Now, look here, miss. I'm a Physics teacher and I'm telling you, there's no way we can slide down that entire slope in one go—or in one piece."

I bump my knee into his. "Nice upgrade. But I'm glad I'm not your student, because you are quite obviously wrong."

Magnus stands up, brushing off his pants and righting his beanie. He holds out a hand in invitation. "I guess I'll have to prove my theory. You game?"

Of course I'm game. Now the forgotten aisle of my memories

has been reopened and the lights turned on in all the nooks and crannies, I'm not about to walk away and forget it again. I'm going to open wide the door from my boring adult main aisle so I won't lose my way. Maybe turn on some music, get a disco ball to go with the chandelier.

And I'm going to prepare a brand new filing cabinet for Magnus. It's going to be tall and green and have lots of little surprises that I can discover when I go exploring. I'll slip the files from that magical night all those years ago into the top drawer.

The memories we're about to make right now will go in the second one. I can already tell they're going to be awesome.

Morbier Impossible

What risks will you take for the perfect bounty?

Mice have no business jumping in parachutes, you say?

I couldn't agree more.

And yet, here I am, about to throw myself into the void with nothing but a piece of cloth tied to my back.

But at the other end, if we succeed on this suicidal mission? The mythical Christmas cheese platter with its deliciously creamy Morbier.

Join the adventure as our hero faces his fears in his quest to put his paws on the perfect Christmas dinner.

Morbier Impossible

I HADN'T REALLY thought I was afraid of heights before this moment. The kitchen table never fazed me, the kitchen counter was easy play, and the top cupboards were easy peasy so long as I stayed away from the edge.

But here I am, in the rafters above the living room, my tail shaking from fear and my paws clutching nervously into the lines in the wood as Lana is explaining for the hundredth time how to work the parachute.

Yes, parachute. On a mouse.

Years ago, Bibi, one of our forefathers—I forget how many generations, I've never been good with numbers—came across a picture in the living room, one of a human falling slowly from the sky and landing safely on the ground. The man wore a helmet and goggles and a backpack for the parachute and was welcomed by his friends with open arms.

Bibi swore he would make the same thing for mice and that it would change their lives drastically.

It certainly changed *his* life; he died when he tested the first prototype.

But before moving into the afterlife of infinite cheese, Bibi passed on his passion for flying to several other mice. The crazy ones. The ones who wanted to get the humans' food from the kitchen table instead of the trash. Who thought mice should have the best parts of the cheese and not just the crust or the moldy bits. The ones who thought baiting and running away from the cat was *a game*.

Unfortunately, having no survival instinct isn't the same as being stupid and they figured out how to make it work. Only lost two more lives during flight tests.

And now, here, today, it's *me* who's supposed to fling myself into the void, with nothing but a flimsy piece of cloth to save me from splattering myself all over the tiled living room floor.

See, as it turns out, human napkins are the *perfect* size for making parachutes for mice.

The research department nicked a whole lot of them from the humans, in different sizes and materials. The paper napkins weren't solid enough, which Huba discovered to his chagrin when he fell to the floor with a splat while the napkin gently flowed down after him, folding in on itself as it did a little dance in the air. The high quality linen napkins were too heavy and didn't hold the air well enough. Cara was more lucky than Huba in that she survived her slow-motion fall but her right hind leg would never be the same.

The cotton everyday napkins were just right. Yuba did a victory dance and was allotted an extra piece of Josephine cheese when he elegantly landed on all four legs after jumping off the old fridge in the basement. The parachute had unfolded itself perfectly, and the strings attached to the four corners of the napkin and Yuba's four legs held without a problem.

The prototype was validated.

Which is how it ended up on my back. I'm in the best team of hunters our family has seen in generations. Our team of four has pulled off the most impressive catches, going from an entire loaf of bread to two choice pieces of Roquefort blue cheese. That last one earned us our names in the hall of fame.

So it seemed natural—to everyone except me, that is—that our team should use the parachutes to pull off the heist of the decade.

See, there's one time of year that is particularly frustrating for a food-loving mouse, and that's Christmas. The humans bring in extra amounts of food this time of year, and it's meatier and fatter and sweeter than anything they eat at any other time.

This does, of course, mean that there is also more leftovers and more waste—but the mice are all too aware of the stuff they're missing out on.

There's a myth that the hunters like to tell each other on cold winter afternoons while they wait for the humans to go to bed so they can start their work. It's the story of Tutu.

Tutu *loved* duck fat. Couldn't get enough of it. Whenever the humans ate duck, Tutu would hang out in the compost for *days*, licking up every last drop of fat. Watching humans eat foie gras was pure torture for him. But nothing, and I mean *nothing*, is guarded as closely as the foie gras. It's impossible to get to and get out alive.

Tutu decided that he didn't care about that last part. He just wanted the foie gras. So on one New Year's Eve, while two humans were preparing the starters for their seven-course dinner, Tutu went hunting in the kitchen.

In broad daylight, with humans right there.

He didn't care. He was in a haze of duck fat and couldn't see farther than the slices of his favorite dish lined up next to litchis, onion jam, and toast.

Rumor has it, one of the humans saw him while he was making his way through the first slice and dropped a mouse trap on his head. The *snap* of the trap could be heard all the way down in the basement and the scream of the human was even louder.

Most mice are able to forego the foie gras. It was Tutu's favorite but he was always a bit weird. But the thing that no mouse can ever stop lusting after?

Cheese.

And what day of the year do the humans buy an *inhuman* amount of the delicious stuff? Christmas. It comes after the salad and before the first dessert. The more people invited for dinner, the more cheese. The calculus department has tried to find an exact correlation for years but hasn't figured out the correct formula yet.

To me, knowing that a lot of humans means a lot of cheese is enough.

And this year, there are a lot of them. At least fifteen according to the last reports of the spymaster.

I'm willing to bet there will be at least ten to twelve different cheeses.

And the mice won't be able to get their paws on any of them. The cheeses always go straight from the refrigerator—which no mouse has ever managed to get into—to a large wooden serving platter that is placed on the rickety old table in the living room corner.

There's no way for a mouse to get *onto* that table. Some have managed to climb up the legs but there's no way to reach the edge of the table top—they always fall to the floor. There's no way to jump onto it from any place nearby—everything is *just* too far away.

The only way onto that table would be from above.

Hence the parachutes.

"Now, remember," Lana tells me as she shoves the end of a string into my paw. "You jump, then you pull—straight away!—and the parachute will open." She's having trouble looking me in the eye because of the helmet falling into her eyes but she doesn't seem to care.

Did you know that hazelnuts are the perfect size to make helmets for mice?

Well, the research department figured it out. Another piece of string under the chin and, *tada!*, we have helmets just like the human in the picture.

Luckily, nobody figured out how to make goggles.

My helmet is chafing on my ears and isn't far from falling into my eyes but I'm not going to take it off. I don't actually *believe* that it will protect me from anything—it's more likely to break my neck than anything else—but I'm also thinking that you never know. What if I find myself in a situation where the helmet *will* save me? So it stays on.

"This isn't going to work, Lana," I say. "That platter stays unsupervised for no more than fifteen minutes so we won't have time for more than one jump. And nobody ever figured out how to steer these things, so the chances of us actually landing *on* the table are, like… Did we not ask the calculus department to look into that? Maybe we should abort."

Lana gives me a distracted pat on the muzzle. "Worst case scenario is all four of us landing away from the table and we'll go home empty-handed. No biggie. Now. Focus. The salad went out five minutes ago—the platter should arrive any minute. We have to get into position."

Our two teammates are on the next beam over. We've decided to spread out because neither beam is *directly* over the table and we have no idea how the parachutes will behave in such a large space.

Jumping off a human-height refrigerator and a two-story-high rafter isn't really the same thing.

Let's not think about that.

Lana sets up as far along the beam as she can get without putting herself in danger of falling off. I stop about a meter ahead of her. We wave the all-clear signal to our teammates and settle in to wait.

It doesn't take long. As there's a surge of noise from the humans at the other end of the large living room, a human with long dark hair comes in from the kitchen.

She's carrying a platter the likes of which I've never seen.

"I count fourteen cheeses," Lana says in awe. "There have *never* been that many before. Holy cheese, I'm hungry."

My mouth waters as I watch the feast approach. The human sets the platter down on the table, adjusts the angle of one of the blue cheeses, and walks back to join the rest of the group.

"All right, people," Lana yells as she signals to our mates. "We have fifteen minutes. Go! Go! Go!"

And she jumps off the wooden beam, her mouth open wide and teeth glistening, her eyes glinting with the high of the hunt.

She pulls on the string—and the parachute unfolds.

On the other beam, I see the two other hunters throw themselves into the void, one with his eyes closed and the other clutching the string in her paw so hard I can see her paw shaking from the strain from where I'm standing.

Three parachutes deployed.

Only me left.

I really, really don't want to do this.

But I can't let my team down, can't let them take all the risks without me. So I close my eyes, make sure I hold the deployment string firmly in one paw—

And I jump.

This is *nothing* like jumping off the old refrigerator.

I can feel the fact that there's nothing solid anywhere around me, just a lot of empty space, and the inevitably approaching hardwood floor. My fur is rippling around my body and the string under my chin is somehow digging into my throat as the helmet tries to act as a parachute.

I pull on the deployment string.

My entire body jerks as the parachute unfolds and my descent is abruptly slowed. Then I'm left rocking gently back and forth and I finally find the courage to open my eyes.

Across the room, the humans around their feast, none of them looking in our direction. Below me, the platter of cheese, already a lot closer than before.

And on my right, a door slamming open.

A gust of cold air sweeps across the room, making several of the humans yell their displeasure at the tall short-haired human coming through the door.

I rock a little under my parachute but nothing too worrisome.

My teammates, however, are not so fortunate.

They take the brunt of the blast from the door. Lana is flung against the wall, her helmet making a dull *clonk* on impact. The parachute deflates partially but it still slows her descent along the wall down to the floor.

She hits the hardwood with a soft squeak.

Nunu is not so fortunate. The gust of wind makes her do several spins around the parachute—up and down at least three times—and when she hits the wall, the parachute deflates completely, making her free-fall from at least as high as the refrigerator in the basement.

She doesn't make a sound. I'm worried.

My last teammate, Enzo, was far enough from the wall to avoid hitting it but he's thrown way off course. He's not going to land on the table.

The door closes and everything calms down. As far as I can

tell, none of the humans have seen the four mice parachuting down on their cheese platter.

I wasn't thrown off course at all by that gust of wind. Quite the contrary, actually.

Moments later, I land lightly smack in the middle of the cheese platter, right on top of the Camembert. A frisson runs up my legs as I feel the soft fur covering the crust under my paws.

I've landed in paradise.

I scramble to unfasten the parachute and as the adrenaline of the flight tapers off, I hear squeaks.

I recognize Lana and her favorite swear words when something goes sideways. And someone's screaming in pain. I can't tell if it's Enzo or Nunu but remembering their descents, it's probably Nunu.

At least she's not dead.

I extricate myself from the strings, jump off the Camembert, and run to the edge of the table to check on my friends.

Enzo has only just landed and is working on freeing himself but is having issues with one of his rear legs.

Nunu is lying by the wall, her parachute still attached and useless, and her small, furry body writhing in pain. Lana reaches her, her parachute still attached to one leg and trailing behind her.

I need to get down there and help them with Nunu.

"Don't you dare come down here without any cheese!" Lana yells at me. "We're taking care of Nunu—you get the food!"

"But…" I shake myself, trying to focus.

The food.

We came here, and took a lot of really big risks, just so we could put our paws on that delicious cheese. Now, here I am, on the fabled cheese platter, but my friend is on the floor in agony.

"We've got her covered," Enzo yells. He has joined the two others and is rapidly untying the parachute strings from Nunu's legs. "*Get the cheese!*"

Fine. I'll get the cheese.

I scramble back to the platter.

There's so much to choose from. Where do I even start?

The large Tomme is out of the question. Even if there had been four of us, we wouldn't have been able to move it. The Roquefort is so mature it's already crumbling. I can get some of it with me but only as much as I can carry in my paws—so hardly any.

There's a Morbier—aw, man, a Morbier—my *favorite* ever cheese. It's creamy and mellow and softer than butter. Its identifying streak of ashes gives it that little extra touch that I just can't resist.

Really, I can't resist.

I run over and nip one tiny piece and gobble it right down.

Then back to work. As much as I love the Morbier, I won't be able to push it off the table all by myself, nor will we be able to get it out of sight before the humans return.

The humans!

I scramble off the platter. There were supposed to be four of us; three for stealing the cheese and one for keeping a lookout. How am I supposed to do everything all on my own?

The humans are still at the table. Some are still eating but for the most part, they're sitting a short distance back from the table, leaning back against the backrests of their chairs, leaving room for their bulging bellies.

My resolve strengthens. I will also have a bulging belly by the end of the night, just you wait and see.

I have to pick a target. As I sprint across the platter several times, I just can't find one that's small enough for me to manage on my own.

Until I hit the goat cheese.

It's *just* the right size. A disk that's maybe a centimeter thick and a little less than my own size across. It's quite light, so I should be able to lift it up on its edge.

I test my theory and find that, yes, I can lift it, then scurry over to the edge of the table to check on my friends.

They've made a stretcher of one of the parachutes and put Nunu inside. Enzo has looped several of the strings over his shoulders and as I watch, he pulls forward while Lana pushes from the back—and the stretcher inches forward.

"Hey, guys!" I yell down at them. "I think I can get a goat cheese. What's the plan?"

Lana looks up at me while pushing. "We have to get Nunu to safety first, but I'll be back to help you repatriate the cheese. Just get it off the table while we're gone!"

The stretcher moves a little faster now and they're aiming straight for the entrance to our lair behind the living room buffet. I scan the room to make sure the coast is clear—

"The cat's coming!"

The panic makes my voice squeak even higher than usual. Nunu would have made fun of me if she wasn't writhing in pain on that stretcher down there.

The cat—that awful, ginormous, diabolical russet-and-brown beast—is standing in the cat door leading to the garage, his blue eyes sharp and his whiskers twitching.

My teammates see him too. None of us dare say another word because the monster's hearing is out of this world. They do speed up, though, pulling and pushing the parachute stretcher across the floor as fast as it will go.

Unless I want to jump down from the table and abandon the cheese, there's nothing I can do to help my friends right now, so although my instincts are telling me to *run! run!*, I scramble back to the goat cheese and get to work.

I push it up on its edge and start rolling it off the platter. It's so simple that I'm wondering if I should attempt a second one.

The cat streaking across the room stops that thought short.

He has spotted the fleeing mice.

And they're so close to safety, too.

Enzo is pulling with all his might, his helmet abandoned halfway across the hardwood floor. Lana's legs are moving so fast, she doesn't get a real grip on the wood and ends up spinning in place.

The cat is already over halfway there.

They're not going to make it.

I scream out the loudest squeak I can.

The cat stops in his tracks, his ears turned toward me.

Clearly having lost all common sense, I stand up on my haunches and wave at him. "Why don't you try to catch me, you great lout? I'm the one stealing the cheese, after all."

On that thought, I give the goat cheese a last push and it goes over the edge.

It lands with a soft splat—it's possible I won't be able to roll it away on the floor as easily as I had across the table.

Then my mind turns to survival, because the cat has accepted my challenge.

He's leaping toward me, murder in his eyes.

I'm about to jump off the table when I see the humans moving. Someone has seen the cat streaking across the room and is wondering what's happening.

If they see a mouse running across the floor, they're certainly not going to be opposed to the cat "doing his job." They'll probably help him do the deed.

If they don't know I'm here, though…

I scramble back to the cheese platter. If I remember correctly…yes! Right there.

The Crottin du Cocumont. Somebody has already cut out a slice. There's room for me to hide. The crust is even the same color as my gray fur so if I'm lucky, it might seem like there's just one big slab of soot-crusted cheese, and no mouse.

I scurry into the V-shaped cut in the cheese just as the cat jumps up on the table and one of the humans shouts out.

I do my best not to move.

At first, the difficulty comes from not shaking with fear. But as my nose realizes where it is, my brain short-circuits.

I'm surrounded by cheese on all sides. It's soft and porous and juicy and just…perfection.

Honestly, if I have to die today, it might as well be here.

I'm starting to understand Tutu and his foie gras.

Careful not to move the rest of my body, I try to cock my

head to nip a piece of cheese—but I'm blocked by the helmet. The stupid, ridiculous hazelnut helmet that they made us wear.

Then I'm ripped back to the present as the entire platter is shaken by the cat's arrival.

"Oh no, you don't!" It's one of the humans who live here. Could my plan be working?

"Shoo! Get off the table! That cheese is not for you, you've got your Christmas dinner in the kitchen. Shoo!"

Lifting my head slightly, I catch a glimpse of the human forcibly lifting the cat off the table, his claws out and his eyes crazy. I'm tempted to wave again but this time I refrain.

"I guess it's time for the cheese," the human says from the kitchen door once she's gotten rid of the cat. "You guys ready?"

Oh no. Being on *this* table is risky enough but if I find myself on the *main* table, where there are over a dozen humans—I'm toast.

I've never moved so fast in my life.

I scramble out of the Crottin and toward the table edge, so much in a hurry that I don't notice one of my hind legs getting caught in the string of my parachute until I'm tumbling over the edge with the thing still attached.

"Oh, good, you thought to remove the evidence." Lana is back and she's all business.

While I try to recover from my fall—fine, I'll admit the helmet finally came in handy—she grabs the parachute and folds it over the goat cheese that's standing just a few paces off. It's now more half-moon shaped than full moon but it's still an entire goat cheese.

"Come on!" she yells at me and starts across the floor with the strings over her shoulders.

I scramble after her and push our bounty ahead of me as we scurry for cover.

"Are those two *mice* pushing a napkin across the floor? Are they wearing *helmets*?"

I almost freeze in fear as I hear the human voice but Lana urges me to keep pushing.

"Don't be daft, Didier. How much have you had to drink?"

"This is only my second glass!"

"Second glass of red. There was the white before that, and the Muscat for the starters…"

The laughter and voices fade away as we push through the hole under the buffet.

We made it.

That night, our names go on the wall of fame for the second time.

It's the first time in recorded history—I checked with the historians—that anyone has brought back *an entire cheese*.

It's only slightly dented and fully delicious and the entire family thanks us as they get a taste.

I've put my helmet up in a niche in the wall and Lana decorated it with some chocolate wrapper she found by the kitchen sink. It looks kind of like the decorations the humans set up for Christmas.

And this year, we also got our feast.

A Second Chance

The Christmas tree stands at the very center of the action during the holidays. It lights the way through the dark, guards the gifts, brings joy.

But once the holidays end and the needles fall, the owners kick the trees to the curb. Quite literally.

Which is where I find them.

I listen to their stories, good or bad. And help them transition into the next phase of their existence.

A Second Chance is a fantasy post-Christmas story about letting go of the past and finding new beginnings.

A Second Chance

Everybody loves a good Christmas tree for Christmas. But once the holidays are over, the trees must go. Nobody wants an old skeleton with twisted limbs and hardly any needles left, standing in the middle of their living room, reminding them that the party's over. So before they go back to work, back to school, back to their everyday lives, they remove the pretty decorations, take down the lights, remove the bright star, and throw the tree out.

Nobody cares what becomes of them.

Most of the time, if they can get away with it, they'll dump the tree anywhere. Even some families who have a fireplace don't go through the trouble of cutting up the tree for firewood. They prefer the wood they bought at the store, which is the right size, and isn't sticky, and won't soil their fireplace. And won't require any physical labor on their part.

In the countryside, the trees that aren't used for firewood usually end up in a ditch, or in the forest, looking up at their living siblings, as they waste away.

In the city, where the risk of getting caught for littering is much greater, most trees are lucky enough to be deposited in a place that will allow them to be recycled.

A place like this.

I stand guard in front of the City Hall, watching over the dying Christmas trees. It is two days before the end of the school holidays, and high season for throwing away Christmas trees.

The city has dozens of these stations, spread out in different neighborhoods and suburbs, in the hopes that people will go to the trouble of bringing their trees. We know from experience that they will not bring them to the waste collection.

Yesterday I brought back over a hundred and fifty trees. From the looks of it, today we'll go over two hundred.

I approach a large fir tree which is leaning against the wooden fence we've set up. She's almost two meters high and has perfect proportions. Her branches still have all their needles, standing to attention. She has no wood boards nailed to her trunk, or signs of having been screwed into a tree stand. The last ten centimeters of the trunk is slightly darkened. She's been allowed a flowerpot, to continue the semblance of life while she served her family.

I brush the fingers of one hand lightly across the needles.

Christmas presents going way above the lower limbs. Two types of white lights; fake candles and falling snow. *Foie gras*, snails in their delicious buttery sauce, beef, potatoes, the traditional *bûche*, and an apple sorbet *trou Normand*—in Armagnac.

I smile at the fir. "You got a good one, huh?"

I lean in and take a good sniff. She smells of wood smoke, long family dinners, and children's laughter. No yelling about going to bed, only long hugs and sweet kisses. No lack of anything, including love.

This fir has lived every Christmas tree's wet dream.

I walk farther down the fence to a pine tree with several broken branches and very few needles left. The pines are usually quite resistant and rarely lose their needles, even after being used as a decoration for over four weeks.

"What happened to you, babe?" I whisper as I trace my hand along one of the broken branches stripped of needles.

Two boys fighting. One probably five years old. The other closer to ten. They're pulling on a fireman's truck, the smallest boy screaming that it's his, his older brother claiming that he can use it as long as his brother isn't playing with it.

The mother coming through the door as the boys crash into the tree. *What are you doing!* she screams at them, her hands coming up, vibrating, next to her head, as if she's resisting tearing out her hair. *Why can't you get along for two minutes? Why do you have to ruin everything?*

The boys, silent in the face of their mother's onslaught, scramble away from the toppled tree. The oldest attempts to straighten the broken branch, but the limb falls down, pointing to the ground.

The fire truck is long forgotten.

You ruined the tree! The boys scoot away as the mother stalks to the trembling pine.

She straightens the branch in much the same way her son has just attempted. When it falls down, she yanks at it, needles falling to the floor. More pulling. *If you can't stay up, you can just get lost.*

But no amount of pulling would break the branch all the way off. So they end up turning the tree to hide the ugly branch in the corner.

Of course, that only worked the first time.

I lean in for a sniff. At least the boys got lots of presents, and not many that they needed to share.

I give the tree a pat. "Don't you worry. You did your job well. And you're not done yet. I'm sure you'll love what we have in store for you."

The bells of the Basilica of Saint-Sernin Basilica ring eight o'clock and I tell my colleague with the large truck to collect the trees. I help him move all the trees into the waiting truck, taking a couple of seconds for each to listen to their stories, giving an encouraging word where it's needed.

Officially, my work ends here. I'm only supposed to collect the trees that people bring me.

But these aren't the trees that really need rescuing.

I get into my little truck and ease down the narrow streets in the direction of the canal.

This is not my first time playing; I know where the lost ones go.

The truck is narrow enough to be able to drive on the cycling path along the canal. I just need to use my key to remove one of the barriers, and off we go.

I don't have to go far before I find the first one. He seems to be a spruce, though it's difficult to tell since only his lower branches and trunk are above water.

A Second Chance

Easing out of the driver's seat, I call out to him. "Don't you worry, honey. I'll get you out."

The poor thing is only a meter or so from the edge of the canal, so I grab a pole with a hook on the end to drag it toward me.

He's a small one. Large and wide branches at the base, but his top doesn't even reach my shoulders. He has clearly been kept up by nailing two planks to his base, but the planks have been removed, leaving only four tiny holes where the nails went in. The branches and needles are in relatively good shape. All in all, he seems healthy. For a tree doomed to die, that is.

I prop the little thing up against the back of my truck and remove my gloves. Shoving them into my back pocket, I reach out to caress the crown.

A crooked star drawn on paper and glued to a piece of cardboard. A metal wire shoved through the star's center and coiled around the very top of the tree. The lines are uneven and the coloring full of holes—the creator can't be more than six years old.

One branch seems to have lost more needles than the others. I lean down to inspect it.

With the smell of tree, and water, and woodsmoke, comes the image of a little girl with long dark hair decorating the tree all by herself. She puts almost all the decorations on this one branch, admiring how pretty it becomes for each item she adds. After a comment—a female voice coming from across the room, apparently from the couch—she adds a few decorations to two or three other branches. But all the while the tree stands in the living room, the little girl only admires this favorite branch.

I inspect other areas of the little spruce, looking for signs of the parents. But I find only the little girl taking care of her tree.

Finally, I lift the tree into the trunk of my truck and put my hand on the base. This is where most people grab the tree when they need to transport it anywhere, especially when it no longer needs to stay pretty.

There she is.

A skinny woman in her early thirties, with long dark, matted hair, dragging the tree behind her as she shuffles along the cycling path by the canal.

Her intention was to go to the Christmas tree round-up where I work.

People are looking at her. Noticing the state of her hair, her clothes. And she's cold. So cold. She should be home in her bed, cuddled into her corner of the couch. Maybe a cup of tea, some chocolate. And her daughter's sweet smiles.

This reminds her of going to work. She used to walk this way to get to the train station. Back in the days when she managed to get out of bed and do something constructive with her time.

She'd get back someday. When she was better.

When she is halfway across the pedestrian bridge crossing the canal, she gives up on her mission and lets the little tree drop into the murky waters below when no one is looking.

The little spruce, only his trunk out of the water, watches his hostess shuffle home to give her daughter a kiss.

"Mmm," I hum to the tree as I make sure he's secure at the back of my truck. "Looks like you had a bit of a challenge, huh? Don't you worry though. You did a great job. You hold onto the memories of your little girl being happy taking care of her Christmas tree. And know that there was clearly lots of love in their household."

Head down, I enter the truck's cab and start the engine. I wish there was something I could do for the woman, but my powers only stretch so far. I'll have to satisfy myself with taking care of the trees, like I always do.

I continue my rounds for a couple of hours, picking up twelve trees from various sidewalks, alleys, and trash cans.

I listen to their stories, tell them they did a good job, and that I have a new task for them.

It's just as I decide to stop for the day that I find the little alien.

I've done this for eight years now, and this has never happened before. I know they exist, of course. Who doesn't. But they don't usually end up on the sidewalk with their living siblings.

He's made of plastic, but the quality is good enough to make him seem lifelike. He's not even perfectly symmetrical, and not because he's been used, but because he was produced that way. He looks like he's covered in snow, but that's also fake, naturally.

He stands here on a street corner, almost as if he's part of the city's Christmas decorations. He stands straight, and is positioned exactly on the corner between two small streets.

I leave my truck behind and approach cautiously. Will this work?

I flick one plastic fake-snow-covered needle with my index finger.

Silence.

I don't always get sound through the visions, but this isn't an absence of sound.

It's a loud, heavy, gray silence. The kind that comes from screaming inside your head. The kind that covers your heart and suffocates it.

I see no decorations, so I move to caress a branch on the opposite side of the tree.

Still nothing. There's a vague memory of lights and angels and shimmering balls, but it's faint, probably from last year. With it comes the image of a man and a woman, slow-dancing without music in front of their tree, the remains of a large meal on the kitchen table.

As I continue easing my hands over the branches, I'm starting to make out some recent surroundings—impressions are more difficult to drag out through the plastic than through living wood, but they're there. He's standing in the corner of the living room, not in the center like he did the year before.

Right next to him: a large cardboard box full of Christmas ornaments.

They never left the box this year.

Most trees give off a whiff of feelings, carried on their scent. To understand them, all one needs to do is not think with words, but with feelings. Let the heart take over from the brain.

This fellow doesn't have a scent, not one his own anyway. But I'm still hearing him, loud and clear.

Sadness. Loss. Frustration.

"What happened, hon? Why didn't you get a Christmas this year?"

Using all my powers and taking my time, I manage to pull the story out of him.

He'd heard them all through the four seasons, from up in the attic—his home for forty-eight weeks of the year.

It started with the woman crying in February. Inconsolable crying for an entire week. Anything could set her off; her husband going grocery shopping, being invited to visit friends, hearing the neighbors reprimanding their kids as they passed in front of the house.

The husband did his best, really. *We'll be all right, honey. We'll try again, and it'll work in no time, you'll see. Why don't we go visit your sister, maybe that'll cheer you up? Of course she won't gloat! Is that really what you think of your only sister?*

Nothing helped, and as the days turned into weeks, the husband's tone slowly went from soothing and sad to something close to accusing and frustrated.

Are you trying to tell me it's my fault? Because this hurt me just as much as it hurt you, you know. But I'm willing to move on.

The wife snapped out of her sadness then. To move straight into anger. *Willing to move on, my ass. You're just willing to get laid.*

And on they went, their barbs hitting closer and closer to the heart, and with increasing frequency.

It took a turn for the worse in August. The husband was away for a week on a business trip when the wife learned of her sister's pregnancy.

She'd not made it to work that week, and managed to alienate most of her family. The little tree heard her on the phone with her cousins and her parents, explaining that her sister had gotten knocked up only to spite her.

Since none of them knew of what had happened in February, they hung up on her. She spent an entire night crying on the floor in the living room, never making it to the bedroom.

When the husband came home, he noticed nothing different.

They only communicated when strictly necessary; to ask the other to take out the trash, or to ask what was for dinner, or to inform of an office party they both needed to attend.

The wife told her husband about her sister's happy news two weeks later. As far as the tree could discern, she hadn't had uninterrupted sleep for more than an hour or two since the last phone call.

I told you about her, she yelled at her husband. *I told you she was evil. Now she's gotten pregnant just to spite me.*

To spite you? Really? You can't even envision her doing it for herself, because it's what she wants for her life? You can't identify with that at all? Really? Who's the father? Is she still with that Matthieu fellow?

Something crashed to the floor, possibly a plate or a mug. *Why can't you ever take my side in anything? What did I ever do to you?*

You're treating me like I don't even exist, that's what! You're ignoring the fact that I'm suffering too. You've retreated into your little bubble and won't ever let me in.

A long silence followed. For the tree, who was used to waiting and not doing anything for months at a time, it was quick, but for humans, it must have been excruciating.

I think you should see someone, he finally said. *A professional. I don't know how to help you on my own.*

She hadn't had an answer to that. In fact, the tree heard not a sound from her for several weeks. They both opened and closed doors, heated water in the kettle, and flushed the toilet. She was obviously there, since her husband talked to her, in a tone of voice usually reserved for mortal enemies, but she never replied or spoke back.

Then, the first week of December, only thirty minutes after the husband had pulled the poor tree down from the attic, and prepared the box of decorations, she spoke again.

I'm leaving.

The tree was out of the dusty attic, finally able to see, but there was nothing *to* see. The wife never came back, and the husband came home from work late at night only to go straight to bed.

This morning, hair about three weeks overdue for a haircut, bags the size of pine cones under his eyes, and breath coming unevenly, the husband had dropped the box of Christmas decorations in the trash and dumped the tree on a street corner on his way to work.

I sigh. "You poor thing," I tell the tree. "You know there was nothing you could do, right?"

I glance back at my truck, its bed filled with abandoned trees. *Real* trees. Which I know what to do with, to give them a new purpose.

But what do I do with a plastic tree?

The glimmer of an idea appears in my mind. In any case, there's no way I can just leave the poor thing here on the street.

The next morning, I'm unloading my catch from the day before at a sawmill some fifty kilometers outside of Toulouse.

"Here we are, my beauties," I say as I line up the trees next to my truck, to give them a clear view of the premises.

"Now, I realize this looks mighty scary. But I'm here to help. Now." I point at the main entrance. "In there is where we're going to cut off the branches."

I'm walking down the line of trees with my hand out, so I can listen to them all in quick succession as I give them my speech. I never try to sugarcoat this part. It's not pretty, it never has been. But there's a purpose behind it, and I need for them to see that, before sending them toward the giant saws.

A couple of the pines emit no more than a sense of resignation. They know they're already doomed to die, might as well be today. A giant spruce toward the end of the line screams out in panic, while a smaller one, the one I fished out of the canal, is silent in confusion.

"I know, I know. Doesn't sound pleasant. And it isn't. But I'm here to tell you it's still going to be worth it."

I have their attention now. I give them an encouraging smile. "Just bear with me for a moment, okay?" I point to a second building. "This is where the larger trunks will be cut into firewood, and the smaller ones together with the branches will be cut into mulch. Yeah, doesn't sound very pleasant, but it's a good thing, honest."

Contemplating the line of beautiful trees in my care, I feel pride rising in my chest. "This means you still have a purpose, see? First, you were growing in the forest. Then, men came to cut you down and sell you for a profit. Then you were adopted by families and helped them create their version of the Christmas spirit. But even though they've now thrown you away, your path doesn't end here.

"The firewood's obvious, isn't it? You'll help some family keep warm next winter. That's an admirable purpose right there.

"And the mulch? It's gonna help make the city pretty. See, it's excellent for helping plants grow in a big city. Big pots of earth let trees grow amid the buildings, but if we just leave the earth exposed, it's gonna harden and sprout an impressive amount of weeds. If we spread the mulch, your remains, on top, it's a protective and nourishing layer, all in one!"

I make another pass down the line. They're contemplative. The large spruce seems proud she'll make lots of firewood. The small one from the canal is remembering a large potted tree he passed on his last trip with his hostess, how happy it had seemed despite the relatively small pot. He liked the idea of helping others grow.

As I signal to the sawmill workers to come get the trees, I let all my pride show on my face to give the trees a boost of confidence.

"I'm very proud of you all. You've grown into gorgeous trees that families wished to share their Christmas with, and you've done your work flawlessly. There's just one last task for you today, which will allow you to be part of something even bigger—the circle of life."

I shut up as the workers drag the trees away. A few years back, two of them overheard me talking to the trees, and they gave me a wide berth for the duration of our collaboration. I don't really care what they think, but want to avoid the trees having the last conversation they hear be a negative one.

Once they're all in the sawmill, I go to the back of my truck. Leaning up against the cab, the plastic tree is all alone.

"As you've probably gathered," I say with a soothing smile, "you don't get off here. Wouldn't be very effective as firewood or compost, I'm afraid." I slap the side of the truck. "But no worries. I've found a job for you, too. Follow me."

Two hours later, we bump down the road to a small cabin in the woods. My neighbor gave me the address; it's apparently a distant cousin of his.

When I exit the truck, a tall, lanky man comes out the front door, closing it behind him. His clothes are worn, but clean, and his face is filled with laugh lines.

"What can I do for you?" he asks as I walk up and shake his hand.

"Your cousin Lionel gave me your address," I say. "I'm hoping you can help me out."

He's wary, but nods for me to continue.

"I work for the city of Toulouse," I say. "I'm in charge of collecting old Christmas trees and getting them recycled."

The man shakes his head. "I'm sorry you've come so far for nothing. We don't have—"

"I know you don't." I smile to make sure he knows I'm in no way judging him for that fact. "But I have a spare."

I wave at my truck, where the little plastic tree is still waiting. "I've a plastic friend who, unfortunately, isn't eligible for recycling, and he's had a rough time of it this past year. I'm looking to find him a new home."

The man's eyebrows shoot up and he glances at my truck. "But…it's January."

I can tell he's interested, though. He's working hard to take care of his family and never break any rules. He couldn't afford to buy a tree, and according to his cousin, he won't even consider cutting down one of the trees in the forest he's living in. The forest isn't his, so it would be stealing.

"Sure." I shrug. "But who says you can only have a tree for Christmas? Most people have to throw them out because they start losing their needles, but a plastic tree? Could stand proud in the middle of the living room all year round."

He licks his lips as he deliberates. His eyes are on the truck, but they flicker back to his house from time to time.

"It's free?" he finally asks.

"Of course," I say. "You're helping me out, honestly. I get kind of attached to the poor things, and I couldn't stomach throwing him in the trash."

He meets my eyes. "Him?"

"Sure." I nod vigorously. "It's definitely a him. He'd probably be really happy if you named him, actually."

"Huh. All right." He chews on his lip some more. "I'll see what the kids think."

I wait outside as he disappears into the cabin for five minutes. I take the time to pull the little tree out of the truck.

"Here you go," I whisper. "This'll be your new home. I have it on good authority that there will be very little yelling here. And there are, like, three or four kids. Maybe you'll even be allowed to work all year round. How about that?"

Its scentless scent carries hope. And joy. And gratefulness.

"You're welcome, buddy. May your life be a long one."

The cabin door slams open, and four kids sprint out. The ages seem to range from two to ten, but they run up to the truck together, the bigger kids helping the smaller ones keep up.

Their eyes go wide when they see the tree.

"It's gorgeous!"

"It's covered in snow!"

"It's almost as tall as Papa!"

I help the father unload the tree and watch as the family brings it into their house. The mother watches from the kitchen window, a baby on her hip and tears in her eyes.

I nod a greeting, then get into my truck. It's almost night, and I need to make my rounds in the streets of Toulouse. The lost Christmas trees need me.

SEVERED TIES

A Ghost Detective Short Story

Depending on the quality of one's company (or the lack thereof), Christmas can be the most wonderful and heartwarming day — or the absolute worst.

And of course, a nice covering of snow never hurts.

Clothilde and Robert never experienced a white Christmas in their thirty years as ghosts. As long as they had each other, nobody complained.

When the latest ghost arrives, buried the day before Christmas, Robert and Clothilde's decades-old traditions for the holiday are interrupted. Their new guest, impeccably polite though he may be, appears to have no desire to address his unfinished business.

Why does he linger if none of it matters to him?

Chapter 1

Christmas is a weird time of the year. It can be the most wonderful and heartwarming days of a person's life, just like it can be the absolute worst. There's no in-between. I think the comparison with the perfect days is the reason the bad ones become so bad.

Being ghosts in a cemetery doesn't really change the phenomenon. Except maybe tip the scales away from the cheer and joy.

Now, don't get me wrong. We're not miserable ghosts by any stretch of the imagination. No moaning, very little spooking visitors, no screaming vengeance at the moon. Clothilde tried that last one at one point in the late nineties but couldn't stay serious for long enough to pull it off.

Clothilde and I have celebrated Christmas together more times than either of us did with our respective families when we were alive, and we've developed our own traditions. A couple of times they were adapted because we had a visiting ghost who hadn't resolved their unfinished business yet, but mostly, it's stayed the same through the years.

It starts with the decoration of the church and the manger. We're lucky enough to live in a cemetery belonging to a church where they put the manger outside. If it was on the inside, we could never have seen it. We're stuck on the outside.

There's a sort of shed a little off to the left of the main entrance. I think it might have been intended as a place to park bikes, by someone who didn't realize very few people ride their bike to church. So it has become the setting for a life-sized manger.

The first time they set it up was our second Christmas here. We were both feeling rather blue, missing our families and not yet come to terms with our status as ghosts, and the fuss of setting everything up and working out the kinks turned out to be exactly the kind of distraction we needed.

Joseph and Maria have been here since that first year, obviously, as has the baby Jesus, one sheep, and one of the wise men. I've never been quite clear on which wise man is which—and neither have the people setting it up because the same mannequin never brings the same gift or wears the same clothes two years in a row—but there wasn't enough money to bring them all the first year. The two colleagues showed up three years later, bringing lots of pretty and sparkling gifts.

Better late than never.

I say Jesus has been here from the start, but the one currently waiting to make his grand entrance on Christmas Eve is actually the fifteenth doll playing the part. It's worrisome how popular it is to steal the baby Jesus. I don't think I want to know what happens to them once they leave sacred ground.

The animals have also slowly trickled in over the years. One sheep became five, soon joined by a donkey and a cow. We only have the head of the cow because making the whole thing would be too costly and take up too much space but all the others are the right size and with the correct number of limbs.

Clothilde and I have been known to spend an evening or two inside the manger, sitting next to the wise men or pretending to ride the donkey, feeling a little less lonely for a few blessed hours.

Once the manger is in place, it's the church's turn. Most of the decorations are set up on the inside, so we never see them, but the porch is usually hung with holly and other twigs and greenery, and live lights are set up along the main path from the parking lot to the church entrance for Mass. On Christmas Eve, more than a hundred lights are lit up all across the cemetery.

It's my favorite moment of the year.

Even though our families aren't here and the people setting out the lights never knew us, it makes us feel remembered.

Tonight is December twenty-third and we're spending the evening in the manger. Outside, it's raining and a nasty western wind is starting up, and even though we can't feel the cold or the wind on our ghostly bodies, we can feel the misery. I've opted to sprawl out on the donkey's hay, with my back against the west wall and my legs crossed at my ankles, while Clothilde is perching on the crib. She usually prefers higher ground but the only other option is on the donkey and she doesn't like that for some reason.

As usual, her legs swing back and forth, passing through the wood of the crib on every swing.

"I'm telling you, that's Balthazar," Clothilde says, eying the mannequin wearing the blue robes and offering a gilded box to the empty crib where the baby Jesus will lie. The box is empty—we checked—but I *think* it's supposed to contain spices of some sort. Unfortunately, I didn't really pay attention to the details of the story of Jesus' birth while I was alive, and access to research materials is woefully slim in a cemetery.

"You're just saying that because it's the only wise man name you know." I eye the box and wonder if I'd even be able to differentiate one spice from another if I still had taste buds. I know I loved cinnamon and clover—but even the memory of their smell eludes me.

Clothilde shrugs. We share a silence—another thing we've become experts at—while Clothilde frowns out at the dreary night. "I wish we'd get a white Christmas for once. Southern France sucks at helping with the spirit of things."

"The last time we had snow for Christmas around here was in 1962," I say. "I was nine." I sigh happily. "It was the most magical night of my life. I made a snowman! Stole a carrot from Maman for the nose and everything."

Clothilde huffs. "I wasn't even born yet. Why couldn't we be buried in the Massif Central or something? I'm sure those guys have snow every Christmas."

The natural answer to that question is, of course, that you don't choose where you're buried based on where there will be snow for the holidays. Your family choose for you, so they can come visit. Except in our cases, we never get any visits. Our families either don't care or don't know where we are.

Neither option is very uplifting.

We fall back into silence. I listen to the drip of rain on the manger's tin roof and the wind rustling the branches of the nearby trees. No other sounds come from the village, not even a car. Everybody is sensibly at home, preparing for tomorrow's big feast.

Until a car pulls into the parking lot, the light of its headlights pouring through the main gate, lighting up the nearest gravestones.

I exchange a glance with Clothilde. It must be almost midnight. Who'd come here at this time of night and in such weather?

Clothilde jumps out in the rain to get a look. The rain falls right through her—the reason we prefer to stay out of the rain because it's such a stark reminder we're no longer corporeal. "It's the hearse. They're bringing someone in."

A funeral the day before Christmas? That's bound to put a damper on the holiday spirit.

Rain be damned, we approach the gate to greet the newcomer. Not a large percentage of dead people become ghosts, so chances are this isn't a new arrival, but we like to accompany the casket through the cemetery anyway. Especially on nights like these.

Two men pull the white casket onto the transportation stretcher and gently roll it toward the church's side entrance. We follow close behind.

"No wreaths," Clothilde comments.

"Maybe they'll come later. They don't always come with the casket."

"*Some* always come with the casket."

I sidestep a puddle even though I can't get my feet wet. Clothilde steps right through it. I like to pretend, she doesn't care.

"The funeral must be tomorrow morning or they wouldn't bring the casket in now," I say. "There's no way they'll be holding the Midnight Mass with a casket up front and center."

Clothilde scoffs. "That sounds like a fun funeral, with the casket surrounded by pretty Christmas decorations and reminders of the party the deceased is missing out on."

It does sound like the perfect way to ruin Christmas for this poor soul's loved ones. For years to come.

One of the men releases the stretcher and goes to unlock the door. "Guess we'll see tomorrow if we have a new ghost," Clothilde says, eying the casket. "Wanna make a bet?"

Ghosts only wake up after the service. Betting on whether or not the dead person has unfinished business and will join us as a ghost is one of Clothilde's favorite pastimes. We have no worldly goods to bet and no possible stakes. Still, it was fun to play for a while. Until I realized Clothilde always won.

"I'm good," I tell her. "Why don't you make your prognostic?"

The two men start pushing the stretcher through the door.

"Nah, I don't think—"

A polite knock sounds from the casket. "Hello?" a gentle male voice says from inside the casket. "Can anybody hear me? I appear to be locked in."

The door closes behind the stretcher and it's just me and a shocked Clothilde in the rain.

Seems like, for once, I should have taken the bet.

Chapter 2

When the casket exits the church the next day, we're ready for him. Clothilde perches on the staircase railing while I lean against the church wall next to the main entrance. The rain stopped around four in the morning and by the time the sun came up, the sky was a clear blue we don't often see around here in winter, and the temperature must have dropped below zero judging by the state of the rare tufts of grass around some of the less maintained graves. As noon is approaching, a couple of clouds are gathering overhead and more forming in the west. It still qualifies as a beautiful day.

"There are, like, five people max attending the service," Clothilde says. "And I haven't seen any wreaths." Her tone is nonchalant, that of a teenager who doesn't care one way or another. I know it's just posturing, though. Clothilde cares, a lot.

And if there's one thing she doesn't like, it's funerals with no loved ones to accompany the deceased to their final resting place.

The fact she probably wasn't accompanied to her own grave *might* have something to do with it.

"We'll see soon enough," I say. They sounded the bells less than five minutes ago, signaling the end of the service. "Do you think he'll come out of the casket straight away?" I ask. I need to distract my friend, but I'm also genuinely curious. "Nobody's ever woken up *before* the service, have they?"

Clothilde shakes her head. "We also usually get screaming and not polite knocking when they wake up."

Yeah, waking up inside a sealed casket? Not fun. Personally, I screamed for days. Don't ask me how it works, but the casket only releases us when we accept we're ghosts. So the duration depends on the person.

The church doors slide open on a creak. I assume a gust of air escapes because a couple of dead leaves blow down the stairs. I can't feel a thing. I straighten and Clothilde jumps down from her perch.

"Hello?" a faint voice says.

Clothilde meets my gaze, baffled. "He's still awake, and still *polite*. How is that even possible?"

I shrug. "I panic when in small spaces. Don't ask me to explain this weird behavior. By all accounts, he should be screaming his head off."

The casket on its stretcher is carried down to the path by six men. One is the priest, and three are cemetery workers we see here regularly. Only two faces are new: a young man in his early twenties with a bright red beanie and a worn bomber jacket, and a woman in her forties with long, salt-and-pepper hair and round, gold-rimmed glasses making her bright blue eyes look perpetually surprised and curious.

"Hello?" the new ghost says again. "Can anybody hear me? I'm not very fond of the dark…."

"Not very fond of—" Clothilde throws her hands in the air. "Nobody is this calm about being dead! That's not human!"

A head pops out of the casket.

Clothilde screams and I skid backward, a hand to my heart even though it hasn't been beating in thirty years.

Without great surprise, Clothilde uses offense as the best defense. "You can't come out of the casket *before* you're buried! You're supposed to crawl out of the ground. Through the dirt. The horror of being buried alive! You can't just *sit* there and say hello like you're a receptionist at a dentist's office."

"Oh." The man turns this way and that, taking in the cemetery and the church. I'd say he's in his mid-fifties, with a huge mop of gray hair and bushy eyebrows. His face is gaunt but there's a kind twist to his mouth and his dark eyes seem to be the keepers of marvelous secrets. I half expect him to invite us into his lap so he can tell us a story.

He's sitting up *through* the casket's lid as if he's in a canoe. Gnarly hands grip the edge—which is a surprise in itself; ghosts usually need some time to learn how to go through some things and on top of others—as he follows the gentle movements of the stretcher toward his final resting place.

"Is this where they're burying me? I must say, it doesn't look so bad." He turns to study me where I'm stumbling along next to the woman with the salt-and-pepper hair, and looks me up and down, taking in my ghostly appearance and the fact I'm walking through gravestones. "Say, Monsieur, would you say this is a decent cemetery to spend eternity in?"

"I, uh…" What am I supposed to answer? "I don't really have much to compare it to." Most people in their thirties don't spend much time in cemeteries—unless they die. In which case you're stuck with the one.

"Yes, of course." He nods to himself before turning to Clothilde.

Clothilde is also keeping pace with the tiny funeral procession, but from a greater distance. I think she's curious—who wouldn't be?—but her expression shows nothing but suspicion. When the man turns toward her, her eyes narrow.

"Delighted to make your acquaintance, Mademoiselle," he says genially. "Théophile Clément, at your service."

Clothilde's expression is nothing short of hilarious. Politeness is not the way to impress girls like her. If she'd still been alive, Clothilde would have been fifty. Clearly, our minds don't age any more than our bodies do once we become ghosts—and doing "old people stuff" is the best way to be ignored by the resident teenager.

Not wanting Clothilde to insult our new friend before he's even out of his casket, I jump in. "That's Clothilde, and I'm Robert. We're the only ghosts in this cemetery at the moment. Tell me, have you been awake for long?"

"Well." Théophile takes another look around, this time taking in the position of the sun and the bare trees of the forest on the north side of the cemetery. "It was Wednesday the last time I went to bed. When I woke up, it was dark and I was in here." He tries to knock on the casket lid, but it turns out to be beyond his capabilities and his hand goes right through. "It's rather difficult to tell time in such places."

"So you couldn't pop your head out until just now?" Clothilde asks. Curiosity is getting the better of her, I'm glad to see.

"I can't say that I tried." Théophile move his hands through the lid, through the side of the casket, holding on to the rim. "I did an awful lot of knocking but I'm beginning to see this doesn't mean much." He tries knocking from the inside. His hand goes straight though. "Huh. It may appear the casket has only recently opened."

Even with years of practice, Clothilde and I can't knock on anything either. We can make it look like we're knocking, but there is never any sound, be it for the dead or the living. The only time a ghost can make a sound—and it's only audible to other ghosts—is when they're stuck inside the casket. I guess even Théophile had to follow that rule.

The stretcher comes to a stop in front of a newly dug grave. The gravediggers came two days ago, so we knew there would be a burial soon, but we weren't expecting it to happen on Christmas Eve. The three cemetery workers help set up the casket, then leave. The priest stands in his usual spot at the head of the grave, while the woman and young man stand at the foot. Given the distance they keep between them, I assume they're not very close.

Théophile observes all this from his perch in the casket. When the priest starts talking, he leans toward me and whispers, "Do you think I should come out now?"

I hold back my laugh. "You might as well. I've never seen anyone halfway out of their casket when it was covered in dirt before. It might not be the best first experience as a ghost."

"Quite." With great care, he stands up, to display he's wearing a classy but worn two-piece suit, the first two buttons of his white shirt open. He hesitates before stepping out, testing the solidity of the casket.

"You can't affect the physical world anymore, old man," Clothilde says. She's found a perching spot on the Gerard family grave in the neighboring plot. "Nor can it affect you. You can walk on air if you want."

Eying the gap between his casket and the solid earth, Théophile doesn't seem convinced. He very carefully takes a long step, going over the side of his casket instead of simply passing through, and finds himself two steps away from the priest—who seems to be doing his usual spiel for the people he knows nothing about.

"Your family couldn't tell the priest anything about you to make this more personal?" I ask.

"My family?" Théophile is brushing down his suit, convincingly enough that ghostly dust particles fall from his trousers.

I point to the woman and young man at the foot of the grave, both staring intently at the casket. No tears, but that's fairly common, all things considered. Not everybody likes to let out all their emotions when out in public.

Théophile's bushy eyebrows draw together. "I've never seen these people before in my life. Why would you make such an assumption?"

Chapter 3

There's nothing like a good mystery to get Clothilde engaged. The minute Théophile tells us he doesn't know his two mourners, she jumps down from her perch and approaches the pair.

She starts with the young man in the red beanie. He stands half a head taller than Clothilde, his hands deep in the pockets of his bomber jacket. Tufts of dirty blond hair curl around the beanie in the back and his deep-set brown eyes stay fixated on Théophile's casket. I don't think he's listening to a word the priest says but I'm willing to bet he's taken note of every single movement the long-haired lady to his left makes.

There's a tension between the two, like either could explode into action at the slightest provocation. I first thought they were members of the same family who had some history.

"I don't think he's had a decent shower in a while," Clothilde comments. "We should probably be glad we don't have a sense of smell, judging by the layer of dirt and grease on his neck."

Beanie-boy must be more sensitive to ghostly activity than most. He lifts a hand to scrub at his neck while he shifts his weight to the other foot.

"Bad teeth, skin that hasn't seen sunblock in years but lots of sun, all of his clothing has seen better days." Clothilde meets my gaze. "I think he might be homeless."

She moves over to the lady. "Doesn't bother coloring her hair to hide the gray. The dress and coat are understated but clean and probably expensive. Those glasses are *gleaming*. It's not possible to have glasses made of actual gold, is it?"

Instead of joining in on the research, Théophile is exploring his new home. Reading the inscriptions on the nearest graves, poking at the plastic flowers on the Gerard plot, gazing beyond the cemetery walls in search of who knows what. When Clothilde mentions golden glasses, he snaps to attention. "Gold is far too heavy for such use. It would be horribly heavy on nose and ears alike."

"Good to know," Clothilde grumbles. Eyes narrowed, she brings her hands to her hips. "If you don't know these two, you might want to help investigating before they leave. Chances are, they're your ticket out of here."

"Ticket out?" Théophile's head whips from one side to the other. Is he looking for a train?

"Only people with unfinished business linger as ghosts," I tell him. With his odd arrival, I haven't even gotten around to doing my usual spiel. "Clothilde and I usually help. Either by figuring out what the unfinished business is, or by finishing it."

"Unfinished business." He says it as if he's trying on the words to see how they taste. "Hah! Hardly surprising I'm there, then. I take it you two would also need decades to tie up everything?"

No, we're still here because we'd need to leave the cemetery to finish our business. Oddly enough, the people who killed us have never come to visit.

Clothilde sneers at Théophile but luckily keeps her thoughts to herself.

"You have a lot of unfinished business, I take it?" I step aside to let the priest access the lift that will lower the casket into the hole without stepping through me. He wouldn't notice—we've met him often enough to know he has no sensibility to ghosts whatsoever—but I hate it.

Théophile goes down on all fours to study the mechanism of the lift. He still hasn't spared his mourners a single look. "I make it a point of honor never to finish anything," he says. "Never saw the point in following other people's orders or bending to their wishes. When I'm done with something, I don't linger. Take high school, for example." He jumps back up and addresses Clothilde directly, for some reason—does he assume she should still be in high school? This won't end well. "Why should I learn by heart the years of such and such battle a random historian has decided were more important than other dates? Why should *they* decide the information to be stored in my brain? I listened to the parts I found interesting and left to do more interesting things when the testing started."

I groan inwardly. I *really* hope this guy will figure out his unfinished business quickly, because I do not want to spend years and years with him here. Clothilde and I get on each other's nerves sometimes, sure, and bored out of our minds quite often. But we're also best friends and we have a routine. I don't want Théophile to mess that up.

So when Clothilde's temper predictably flares and she stalks away from the two mourners to follow up on Théophile's comments, I take her place. Logically, the answer to our prayers should be with these two. If I could only get them to talk.

Before I can even decide on a line of attack, the woman with the golden glasses turns slightly and gives the young man a once-over. Although the two have clearly been acutely aware of each other throughout the ceremony, this is the first time either has looked at the other.

The man in the red beanie's eyes twitch in her direction but turn back to the lowering casket before their reach their destination.

"She looks like a nice lady," I say to him. "It might be a good idea to talk to her. Figure out what her link to Théophile is."

Live people can't hear us, but the ones who are sensitive to otherworldly activities can somehow absorb what we say to them anyway. I think their subconscious can hear us and brings our words up as ideas to their own minds. Unfortunately, it's not an exact science, but we make do. It's the only way we have of solving dead people's mysteries around here.

The young man's sensitivity is confirmed when he turns to face the woman. "I'm Xavier," he says in a rough voice. "You knew him?" He nods toward the grave.

The casket is at the bottom and the priest has thrown in his handful of dirt. It seems neither of the mourners have the intention of doing the same and the priest is awkwardly rounding things up so he can leave and get ready for the Midnight Mass. Clothilde is listening to Théophile talk and the way her eyebrows are reaching for the sky is not promising.

The woman's face flickers with what I think is disappointment. "I'm Mathilda," she says and holds out a hand. "And yes, I had the misfortune of knowing Théophile."

Xavier lets out something between a huff and a sigh as he reluctantly shakes her hand after wiping it off on his pants. "I take it I'm not the only one he disappointed in life?"

Clothilde comes stomping to join us, while Théophile seems to be aiming for the nativity scene. The spring in his step is nothing short of joyous. Is it possible to be happy to be dead?

"The guy takes *pride* in disappointing people," she almost growls. "If anyone ever shows the slightest indication of expecting anything from him, he's out. Nobody but Théophile dictates what Théophile does."

I acknowledge what she says with a nod but don't make a reply. I want to hear what Mathilda has to say to Xavier.

"Théophile leaves a *long* trail of disappointed people behind him." There's compassion for the young man in her tone but also a hardness that I'm guessing is especially fitting when talking about our newest ghost. "You shouldn't feel bad about it; it has nothing to do with you personally."

Xavier doesn't look like he believes her, but he keeps silent and burrows deeper into the collar of his jacket. More clouds have blown in during the burial and the lack of sun is probably felt keenly by those who still have corporeal bodies.

"Besides," Mathilda continues, "I'm guessing you're here because you got something from his estate? Nobody else would even know about the funeral."

I'm starting to understand the lack of wreaths and mourners.

Xavier nods. "I've apparently inherited a house." He doesn't seem to quite believe his own words. "Nothing is done according to the current norms because he didn't believe in following rules, but it's still a house. A nice one." His voice cracks on the last words.

"Indeed it is." Mathilda reaches out to pull on Xavier's elbow and the pair walks slowly toward the parking lot. Neither spares as much as a glance at the grave. Clothilde and I trail behind, listening in. "If you got the house, I assume it's because of law and not something Théophile did?"

A curt nod.

Mathilda pushes her glasses up her nose. "Me, I officially got the half of my business that Théophile still owned. I've managed everything for ten years and he never helped or bothered me, so it won't actually change much. But it's nice to know it's all officially mine."

"We can't let them leave without figuring out what that jerk's unfinished business is," Clothilde says as we approach the gate. Ghosts can't go past that barrier.

"It seems unfinished business is what he does," I reply. "But if it doesn't bother *him*, why would it be keeping him here? There has to be something—hopefully *one* thing—that's unfinished even in his mind."

Two steps from the gate, the young Xavier stops. His gaze is distant and his breath is short. "He's the reason my life is so miserable," he says to his feet. "It's because of him my mom overworked herself so much she didn't realize she had cancer before it was too late. He starts something, gets everybody around him excited to go with him, then drops everything and leaves. At the worst possible time." His anger is taking over, his voice rising and his posture becoming less cowed.

Mathilda nods in understanding and patiently waits for the rest.

"He left two days after I was born," Xavier spits out. "When the hospital staff told him it was his job to do the paperwork to officially name me. Add in my mom expecting him to keep their business afloat for a month and he was gone.

"The jerk was my dad."

Chapter 4

We watch as the taillights of Mathilda's car disappear down the road. Xavier was on foot but accepted her offer of a ride to his new home. According to the clock on the church it's mid-afternoon, but it's almost dark already. There's not a speck of blue sky in sight, only heavy, dark clouds. It looks like we're getting a wet and depressing Christmas.

In the company of the most selfish ghost I've ever encountered.

"Having a kid should be important to anyone, right?" Clothilde says. "Even self-centered liars?"

I look toward the church and spot Théophile in the manger, apparently studying the craftsmanship of the cow. "I certainly hope so," I reply on a sigh. "At least it gives us an angle of attack. Except, if his business *is* with his son, I have no idea how we're going to resolve it. I doubt that man is ever coming back here."

Her jaw jutting out with hardened resolve, Clothilde marches toward Théophile like a general going to war. "The issue will be resolved in *his* head. And we're going to figure out how. I'm *not* spending eternity with that loser."

When we reach him, Théophile is riding the donkey, a joyful smile on his face. "It's a shame I can't feel the fur. It looks wonderfully soft."

"You lied to us." Clothilde crosses her arms and widens her stance. If she hadn't been wearing her usual ankle-length jeans and flowing white blouse, she'd look downright intimidating. "You said you didn't know either of your mourners."

By the way his nose tips up and his hands smooth down his vest, I can tell he's going to deny it. Which I don't have the patience for today, so I speak before he can. "The woman was a business associate of yours. It's kind of hard to forget someone you work closely with."

Théophile sniffs. He seems to be about to deny everything, gets a look at Clothilde's furious face, and deflates. "Fine. I knew Mathilda. But I don't see why she'd show up to my funeral. There was no love lost between us. The young man, I've never seen before, though."

"You left him and his mother when he was two days old," I say. "I suppose it's reasonable to assume he's changed since then. Especially since he appears to have been homeless for some time."

That does the trick. Théophile forgets he was sitting on the donkey and is suddenly standing a foot off the ground, halfway through the stuffed animal. He's been quite adept at being a ghost this far, but everyone has their limits.

"That was David?" he asks. His voice is almost uncertain.

"Oh, God, you have even more kids you've run out on?" Clothilde throws her hands in the air and pretends to choke Théophile from afar.

Théophile straightens, and when he realizes he's floating mid-air, drops to the ground. His nose is in the air again. "I have not 'run out on' more than one boy, I assure you. Just the one, about twenty years ago. And his name was David."

"Except you refused to do the paperwork to name him," I say. "And I'm guessing the mom decided *she* wanted to decide the name, since she was the one who had to do everything after you left. His name is Xavier."

"Xavier! But that's— Oh. Well, then." He crosses his arms only to uncross them immediately.

"Would we be right to assume your unfinished business is with your son?" I ask.

"Why would it be about him? I've always made a point of never finishing anything."

"Yes, so we've understood." I glance at the mannequins of Mary and Joseph, already set up so they hover over the empty crib where Jesus will appear tonight. Without the baby, they look kind of sad, like they're happy about a pile of hay while ignoring everybody else around them. Once the baby is in place, though, they'll be equal parts happy and worried parents. Like I imagine most parents feel when they look down on their newborn for the first time.

"Still. Leaving your son behind can't sit entirely right, even with someone used to disappointing everyone around him?"

Théophile huffs. "I don't understand why he was here at all."

"Clearly, the mother did *her* work well, and listed you as the father. The boy just inherited your house, and probably most of your belongings."

The shock of this news is so strong Théophile's ghostly form flickers. I have a second to hope it means he's moving on, but then he comes back.

Clothilde cackles. "Shocked the state helps you take care of your kid, Théophile? It's very hard to leave your children with nothing in France. And if you don't have a will, they get everything. A case where doing nothing actually is doing something."

That shuts him up. I'm not sure if he needs time to reflect on his life and his choices or if he's avoiding us, but he spends the rest of the afternoon walking the cemetery, discovering his limitations as a ghost. Clothilde and I stay in the manger, chatting about the wise men and their gifts. Maybe we could drop a hint with one of the ladies who set it up for them to properly label the gifts? Twenty years of asking ourselves the same questions get a bit tedious.

When the bells strike nine thirty, people start filing in. Some come by car, quite a few on foot. Most families will start their Christmas feast once they get home, but the ones with very young children have probably already dug into the foie gras. I remember the taste well enough to know I miss it.

We stay in the manger, Clothilde perched on the donkey and me sitting on the floor next to Joseph. This way, when the churchgoers come to check out the nativity scene, it almost feels like they're talking to and seeing us.

Every year, I study every single person passing through the church doors. I know we're not far from the village where I grew up and where part of my family presumably still lives, and I cling to the faint possibility they would come here for Midnight Mass one year. If they do, I don't want to miss it.

This is probably why my first reaction to seeing Xavier and Mathilda show up again is jealousy.

Théophile spent his entire life running from everything—and yet they come back for him.

"Théophile!" I yell into the night. "You have visitors!" An old couple by the stairs startle, and after a shared look, hurry inside the church.

Théophile appears and when he sees his son, goes straight to him. The pair has stopped some distance off, apparently arguing whether or not to attend Mass. Although I frankly don't want to, I saunter over to join them. This *is* our best chance at getting rid of Théophile.

"We've already listened to the priest's yapping once today," Xavier says on a sigh. "Isn't that enough?"

"It's Christmas and you're going home to a feast of buttered pasta for one," Mathilda says with a kind smile. "You can afford to listen to the words of a kind man for an hour or two."

"There's a box of foie gras somewhere in the basement, if you can find it," Théophile says to his son. His voice is distant and the way he's looking at Xavier is very intense. I think he might be trying to see himself in the young man.

"Maybe I'll have a look around in the basement," Xavier says. "See if the old man had any treats hidden away."

Théophile whips around to stare at me.

"Your son is sensitive to ghosts," I tell him. "If you have something to say to him, he might even hear it." As if the man is ready for something as decent as an apology.

"Hey, look," Mathilda says, and points to the sky. "I think it's snowing."

At first I think she's simply trying to get Xavier to think of something else, until a snowflake lands on the young man's nose and promptly melts.

Clothilde appears at my side, her face even more youthful than usual. "It's snowing? For Christmas? Really?"

I can't help but laugh. "Looks like it. Go enjoy your first white Christmas, Clothilde."

On a happy laugh, Clothilde does just that.

Xavier seems equally happy. He tips his head to the sky and closes his eyes, letting the snow fall on his face. "And I'll have a warm bed and a roof over my head tonight," he whispers.

Théophile is the only one in the group who doesn't care about the snow. He's so close to his son's face, it borders on creepy. It's a good thing only us ghosts can see him. "That's not right," he says. "How can a son of mine fall so low he doesn't even have a roof over his head?"

"Maybe he didn't inherit your lack of empathy and sense of community," I say.

Théophile falls silent but doesn't stop his fierce scrutiny of his son. Around us, people are exclaiming about the snow, some happy, some worried about getting home after Mass.

"I didn't know how to be a father," Théophile says. His eyes are still on his son, but I think he's talking to me. "He was better off without me. I would have messed him up, like I do everything. It's no great issue when you mess up a business deal or a friendship. But a fragile, little life? I panicked." He reaches out to touch his son's cheek, but lacking practice, he goes right through. "I did what I thought was best for you, Dav—Xavier. Really."

The young man definitely hears his father. He turns to gaze toward the newly dug grave across the cemetery. "I guess I should thank my father for the house," he says. "He hasn't done anything for me while he was alive, but at least dead, thanks to him, I'll be warm tonight."

Mathilda sighs and gives him a hug. "If I needed a proof you're his son, that kind of whacked-out logic will do it. But yes, let's look at the positive side. You have a warm place to sleep tonight, and every other night this winter, and we get snow for Christmas!"

The pair walk into the church and soon, the doors shut behind the last of the revelers. Outside, in the snow but leaving no footprints, stand three ghosts. And let's not forget the mannequins of the nativity scene.

"Seems you managed to help your son, after all," I say to Théophile, who appears to be frozen in place as he stares at the spot where his son disappeared into the church. "Better late than never?"

His confused eyes meet mine. "I helped him?" There's definitely hope in his tone.

"I'd say so. Giving a home to a homeless person definitely qualifies as helping."

"Huh." His eyes go back to the church doors and as a huge smile grows on his face, his body becomes more and more transparent.

I open my mouth to tell him goodbye, or to point out he's finished his business, but in the end I stay silent. I don't want to interrupt the obvious happiness he's feeling. I hope he gets to take it with him wherever he's going next. Despite having been a rather despicable human being, he must also have been very lonely. Finishing off knowing he helped his son feels right.

Five minutes later, an excited Clothilde comes back. "Where'd the jerk go?"

"He moved on."

"Really? That was quick." There's a slight hint of envy in her tone, but I know it won't linger. We're used to being just the two of us and can take years more while we wait our turn.

I'm just glad we don't have to wait with Théophile.

One of the church ladies slips out the side door with a bundle in her arms.

"Ah, here comes the baby Jesus."

So we hold up our own Christmas tradition. We sit with Mary and Joseph as their baby is "born" and watch our cemetery being quietly covered in a blanket of snow with the congregation singing Christmas carols inside the church.

"I've always wanted a white Christmas," Clothilde says happily as she gives the Jesus doll a pat.

See? No need for fancy gifts to have a perfect Christmas.

Author's Note

THANK YOU FOR staying with me for these short holiday stories. I hope you enjoyed them!

The Magic of Sharing was first published in the 2020 WMG Holiday Spectacular, and *Severed Ties* was in Issue #15 of Pulphouse Fiction Magazine in December 2021. I'm always thrilled when one of my stories find a home in one of WMG's projects.

If you enjoy short stories, I have several collections you can try out. *A Thief in the Night* and *Deep Dark Secrets* hold five mysteries each, while *Unfinished Business* contains the first five Ghost Detective stories, and *Tales From the Trenches* holds Young Adult stories. A little something for everyone!

To make sure you're in the loop of all new releases, remember to sign up for my newsletter on my website.

R.W. Wallace
www.rwwallace.com

About the Author

R.W. Wallace writes in most genres, though she tends to end up in mystery more often than not. Dead bodies keep popping up all over the place whenever she sits down in front of her keyboard.

The stories mostly take place in Norway or France; the country she was born in and the one that has been her home for two decades. Don't ask her why she writes in English—she won't have a sensible answer for you.

Her Ghost Detective short story series appears in *Pulphouse Magazine*, starting in issue #9.

You can find all her books, long and short, all genres, on rwwallace.com.

Also by R.W. Wallace

Mystery

Ghost Detective Novels
Beyond the Grave
Unveiling the Past
Beneath the Surface
Piercing the Veil

Ghost Detective Shorts
Just Desserts
Lost Friends
Family Bonds
Common Ground
Till Death
Family History
Heritage
Eternal Bond
New Beginnings
Severed Ties

Ghost Detective Collections
Unfinished Business, Vol 1

The Tolosa Mystery Series
The Red Brick Haze
The Red Brick Cellars
The Red Brick Basilica

Short Story Collections
Deep Dark Secrets
A Thief in the Night

Romance

French Office Romance Series
Flirting in Plain Sight
Hiding in Plain Sight
Loving in Plain Sight

Standalone Novels
Love at First Flight

Holiday Short Stories
Down the Memory Aisle
Morbier Impossible
A Second Chance
The Magic of Sharing
The Case of the Disappearing Gingerbread City
The Lucia Crown
Crooks and Nannies

Young Adult

Short Story Collections
Tales From the Trenches

Find all R.W. Wallace's books:

rwwallace.com/allbooks

www.ingramcontent.com/pod-product-compliance
Lightning Source LLC
LaVergne TN
LVHW032006070526
838202LV00058B/6315